BIG .70

Now that he thought of it, the "undertakers" had arrived before Dunston's group, unloaded the coffins, and had gone to the sidelines and stayed there, ignored and unnoticed . . .

Their opening shots signaled Parry's charge. The outlaws spurred their horses, sweeping up the hill into the graveyard. The undertakers swung their guns downhill. Dunston was a dead man, unless—

The Big .70 roared.

Crashing like thunder, it punched a hole in the nearest undertaker. Ejecting the spent shell, Boyd fed a fresh round into the breech.

Thunder hammered again, letting daylight into the second gunman . . .

DON'T MISS THESE
ALL-ACTION WESTERN SERIES
FROM THE BERKLEY PUBLISHING GROUP

THE GUNSMITH by J. R. Roberts
> Clint Adams was a legend among lawmen, outlaws, and ladies. They called him . . . the Gunsmith.

LONGARM by Tabor Evans
> The popular long-running series about U.S. Deputy Marshal Long—his life, his loves, his fight for justice.

SLOCUM by Jake Logan
> Today's longest-running action Western. John Slocum rides a deadly trail of hot blood and cold steel.

McMASTERS by Lee Morgan
> The blazing new series from the creators of *Longarm*. When McMasters shoots, he shoots to kill. To his enemies, he is the most dangerous man they have ever known.

McMASTERS

BIG .70

LEE MORGAN

J

JOVE BOOKS, NEW YORK

If you purchased this book without a cover, you should be aware that this book is stolen property. It was reported as "unsold and destroyed" to the publisher, and neither the author nor the publisher has received any payment for this "stripped book."

BIG .70

A Jove Book / published by arrangement with
the author

PRINTING HISTORY
Jove edition / December 1995

All rights reserved.
Copyright © 1995 by Jove Publications, Inc.
This book may not be reproduced in whole
or in part, by mimeograph or any other means,
without permission. For information address:
The Berkley Publishing Group, 200 Madison Avenue,
New York, New York 10016.

ISBN: 0-515-11765-X

A JOVE BOOK®
Jove Books are published by The Berkley Publishing Group,
200 Madison Avenue, New York, New York 10016.
JOVE and the "J" design are trademarks
belonging to Jove Publications, Inc.

PRINTED IN THE UNITED STATES OF AMERICA

10   9   8   7   6   5   4   3   2   1

BIG .70

One

On an October morning, Boyd McMasters got off the train at Flagstaff, Arizona. Long and lean, with a weatherbeaten face, he was dressed as a townsman in a black broadcloth suit, white shirt, and string tie. He had two pieces of luggage: a carpetbag and a long narrow carrying case. The case was about six feet long, almost as tall as he was. He carried it under his left arm. The carpetbag was held by the grips, in his right hand.

He bought a stagecoach ticket for Smoke Tree in Sinagua County, some fifty miles south. His gear was stowed in the back boot of the coach. A strongbox was loaded up top, and the stage moved out.

The landscape was flat, dry, with mountains in the distance. The six-horse team kicked up plenty of dust. The coach rattled, shook.

The driver was Ned Tipton; big Butch Randle rode shotgun. The passengers were Boyd, Meg Kerner, Mary Sue Curry, Clarissa Bane, and Cy Sandiford. Meg Kerner had gotten off the train at Flagstaff too. She was thin, fine-featured, and coughed a lot. She had been met by her aunt, Mary Sue Curry, who was escorting her to Smoke Tree. Mary Sue was middle-aged, dish-faced. Clarissa Bane was a beauty, red-haired, green-eyed, full-bodied. Cy Sandiford was jowly, with frizzy hair and a ginger-colored walrus mustache. He wore a derby hat and loud checked suit. He claimed to be an investor, but everything about him said "tinhorn."

Boyd introduced himself. "I'm Frank Bowman," he said "I hope to drum up some business in Smoke Tree."

Sandiford said, "What's your line, Mr. Bowman?"

"Ranch improvements," Boyd said.

Which was true, as far as it went.

The road stretched south across the Coconino Plateau, through thick pine forests. The air was heavy with a resinous piney scent, drowsy and aromatic. The route descended the south slope, spilling into Oak Creek Canyon, running parallel to the west bank of the creek. The pines thinned out on the open flat, replaced by clumps of cacti and scrub brush which dotted the gray, brown, and tan landscape. Human habitations were few and far between.

In late afternoon, the stagecoach stopped at a swing station, picking up a fresh team before continuing south.

The sun went west, shadows stretched east. The hard-packed road vibrated like a drumhead beneath pounding hooves and clattering wheels. The passengers were hot, dusty, and tired. Rocky spurs thrust out of the ground, sandstone islands the color of red bricks. On both sides of the road sprouted a forest of spires, eroded into weird, twisted shapes.

The sun set, leaving behind golden light and purple shadows. Every pebble, every blade of grass stood out clear and distinct. Light faded, shadows deepened. It was still hot. Venus shone above the western horizon.

The road dipped and rose, dipped and rose. The troughs deepened and the crests became higher. Mountains hemmed in the road. The stagecoach wound steadily upward, snaking around stone pinnacles, climbing into the hills.

Nightfall. A bright half-moon rose, flooding the scene with silver light. Mountains were outlined with crystal clarity, their shadows inky-black.

Ahead loomed Sinagua Plateau. The stagecoach started up the grade. The team labored along the switchbacking road, now little more than a trail. Progress slowed to a crawl. Harnesses creaked, hoofbeats plodded.

The stagecoach wormed its way to the heights. The flat was far; the summit near. On the inside, the trail was bounded by rock walls; on the outside, empty air.

The coach tilted to its steepest angle yet, almost halting. Tipton cracked the whip, urging the team onward. Butch Randle cursed. A wheel struck a rock, sending it over the edge. It was a long time falling before striking faint, distant echoes far below.

Meg Kerner gasped. Mary Sue Curry squeezed her niece's hand. Sandiford sucked at an uptilted pocket flask, forgetting he'd drained it long ago.

The coach crested a rise, setting all four wheels on level ground. The passengers let out the breath they'd been holding.

The plateau was a thousand feet above the flat, itself

four thousand feet high. The summit was a vast shallow basin, bounded on the west by a saw-toothed mountain range. Somewhere in the peaks a river rose, snaking across the basin floor before spilling over the southeast rim to feed the Verde River far below.

The stagecoach was in North Pass, a notch in the rock-rimmed lip of the basin. The road sloped downward along the gently curved inner wall. The tableland was shot through with silver veins: moonlight reflecting on the watercourse. In the distance was a yellow smudge, the lights of Smoke Tree.

Going downhill, the horses stepped easier, more sprightly. The shallow slope was littered with boulders. The air was cool, with the smell of green growing things.

The road flattened into a long straight stretch.

The coach slowed. A shot sounded, along with the thud of a bullet striking flesh. A meaty thud, like a pickax striking a side of beef.

The coach stopped, throwing the passengers from their seats.

A heavy object hit the ground on the right side of the coach, triggering a shotgun blast.

The horses reared, whinnying, stamping.

More shots sounded, a ragged fusillade. Muzzle flares flashed in the darkness, a stone's throw from the right side of the road.

Tipton said, "God!"

A voice said, "Throw down the strongbox!"

It was hard to hear, over the noise of the horses. The speaker said, "You won't be hurt! We just want the cash!"

Tipton said, "You killed Butch, you sons of bitches!"

A shot struck the coach, near the driver. A second voice said, "We mean business!"

Boyd said, "Drive, man!"

Sandiford said, "Why don't he go?" He pulled a gun from his jacket pocket, a short-barreled nickel-plated revolver.

Boyd said, "Go, damn you!"

Tipton said, "I can't! Road's blocked!"

Sandiford fired a shot. The robbers returned fire. Muzzle flares spiked, betraying their position. Three, at least, centered around a clump of trees.

Slugs tore through the side of the coach, spraying splinters. The women huddled on the floor.

Boyd's gun was in his hand. Sandiford fired some more, doing no damage. Deafening gunfire filled the coach with smoke.

A figure rose crouching from behind a rock, angling for a clear shot. Boyd shot him.

The robber flopped backward, crying, "I'm hit!"

The other two poured it on. Sandiford had to reload. He leaned back, flattening himself against the seat while fishing out a handful of loose shells from his pocket. A slug took a bite out of the window frame inches from his head. He dropped the shells.

"Damn!" he said.

Boyd squeezed off some shots at the robbers. He didn't hit them, but he broke up their timing. Only two shooters now. The third man's gun had been silent since he was hit. He thrashed around behind some rocks, bawling and moaning.

Sandiford's coat pocket yielded more shells. He fed them into the chambers.

Clarissa Bane started to rise from the floor. Her eyes were wide, her face white and strained. She held a derringer, a neat little twin-barreled job.

Boyd said, "Save it for if they get close."

She nodded.

His gun was empty. He holstered it. He had another one, stuffed butt-out in his waistband over his left hip. He drew it, telling Sandiford, "Cover me!"

Sandiford threw some lead at the robbers. Boyd opened the left side door of the coach and hopped out, crouching low.

Beyond the edge of the left side of the road lay a patch of open ground covered by a bed of prickly pear cactus. That explained why it was free of robbers. Tipton hung by his hands from the top rail of the roof on the coach's left side, still holding the reins. Butch Randle lay slumped on the ground near the right front wheel, still clutching his shotgun. Moonlight glistened on the bloody exit wound between his shoulder blades.

The wounded outlaw was screaming and crying. "Oh Gawd, I'm hurt bad—!"

The horses were half-mad from gunfire, blood, and death. They pawed the earth, kicking up dust. Why didn't they bolt and run?

In the middle of the road lay a dead tree, blocking the way.

The wounded man bellowed, "Help me, boys!"

"Shut up!" a robber said.

"It hurts!"

A bullet smashed a spoke of the left rear wheel. Sandiford shot at the shooter. Boyd moved forward, shielded by horses and dust.

The dead tree was forked, man-sized. Dead leaves clung to its branches. Boyd held his fire, not wanting to betray his position. He put away the gun, grabbing a tree limb with both hands.

The tree didn't want to move. He dug in his heels, straining. It moved a few inches. It must have weighed a couple hundred pounds.

Something tugged the flap of his coat—a bullet. Another hummed past his head. A third struck the tree, shivering it, pulverizing a fist-sized chunk of dead wood.

The shots all came from the same gun. An excellent motivator! When Boyd heaved at the tree again, it damned well moved. He swung it to the side, like opening a gate.

The horses broke when they saw open road. The stagecoach lurched forward. Tipton was in the driver's seat, hauling back on the reins. There was no stopping the maddened beasts, but he managed to slow them enough for Boyd to catch hold of the stage as it rumbled past.

Boyd clung to the door frame, feet in the air. Beneath him the ground was a blur of motion. He scrabbled for a toehold, finding none. Pain stabbed deep into his shoulder joints, but he kept his grip.

Hands reached out from the coach, hauling him inside.

The robbers fired at the fast-dwindling coach but did not pursue it.

The stagecoach tore into Smoke Tree. People ran to get out of its way. Tipton threw the handbrake and reined in the team. The stagecoach stopped at the crossroads in the center of town.

A crowd gathered. Tipton fired some shots in the air, shouting, "They've killed Butch!"

More people came running: cowboys, miners, townfolk. It was nine o'clock at night. The curious clustered around the coach, milling, buzzing.

Boyd got out of the coach. He was bareheaded, having lost his hat during the holdup attempt. Gawkers shouted questions at him. He stood off to the side, smiling, saying nothing. He smiled with his lips closed. The smile ended above his mouth. His would-be interrogators gave it up as a bad job and tried to pump the other passengers instead.

The road from the pass ran north-south across the basin, becoming Grand Street where it ran through town. Buildings lined the street on both sides, wooden-frame structures, stores and saloons mostly, fronted by plank sidewalks. Horses lined the edges, tethered to hitching posts. Flies buzzed the manure piles.

The buildings grew bigger and more elaborate closer to the main cross street, Mercado Street. The junction of Grand and Mercado was the heart of town. Despite the hour, Smoke Tree was open for business: whiskey business, girl business, gambling business.

Windows were ablaze with light, illuminating the crossroads in the absence of street lamps. Overhead, a smoky red glow flickered.

Somebody said, "Here comes the sheriff!"

Sheriff Wade LaRue wore a brown hat, brown suit, and tan vest. He had a long seamed face and a pencil-thin black mustache. He was trailed by his deputy, Cliff Olcott. Olcott was big, oxlike, with little piggy eyes.

LaRue was wild-eyed, agitated. He made a beeline to

Clarissa Bane, embracing her.

"Thank God you're safe!" he said.

When he finally broke out of the clinch, he looked much better. Boyd didn't blame him. A double armful of Clarissa Bane would be a tonic for any man's nerves.

A chaw of tobacco bulged in the corner of Olcott's jaw. He spat out a glob of juice and said, "What's all the fuss?"

Tipton said, "Outlaws tried to hold up the stage! They killed Butch Randle!"

LaRue excused himself from Clarissa, crossed to Tipton, and grabbed him by the arm. He said, "Butch—dead?"

"Yessir! He never had a chance, Sheriff! They shot him down like a dog!"

Olcott said, "A shame. They get the payroll?"

The miners in the crowd pressed forward. One of them said, "Yeah, what about the payroll?"

"They didn't get it," Tipton said.

LaRue said, "Who was it, Tipton?"

"I don't know, Sheriff! It was too dark to make 'em out. There was three of 'em, though."

LaRue didn't like that answer. Olcott said, "Can't identify them, eh?"

Tipton shook his head. "But we got one of 'em!"

LaRue liked that better. "Dead?"

"Hurt bad," Tipton said.

"Good."

"One of them fellows got him," Tipton said, indicating Sandiford and Boyd.

The lawmen eyed them. LaRue wasn't through with Tipton. He said, "Where's Butch?"

"Back at North Pass."

"You left him there?"

Tipton swallowed hard. Boyd said, "He was dead, Sheriff. I saw him."

Tipton nodded, grateful for the help. The lawmen turned to face Boyd. LaRue said, "And who might you be?"

"Bowman, Frank Bowman," Boyd said.

"You shot the outlaw?"

"Mr. Sandiford here and I were both shooting. I don't know which of us got him. It was a lucky shot."

"Much obliged, whoever did it," LaRue said.

Solemnly he shook hands first with Boyd, then Sandiford. Olcott kept his hands to himself.

LaRue said, "Anyone hurt? Besides Butch, I mean."

"No, sir," Tipton said.

Meg Kerner lay stretched across one of the coach seats, gasping and wheezing, while her aunt fretted over her. LaRue said, "What's wrong with her?"

Tipton shrugged. "She ain't hit, is all I know. Throwing a fit maybe."

LaRue said, "Send for Doc Grinnell."

"He's on the way," somebody said.

LaRue spoke to his deputy. "Time's a-wasting, Cliff. Round up the boys and let's get after those killers."

"They've got a pretty good start."

"That wounded man will slow them up some. We'll steal a march on those damned Hulls too."

A disturbance rippled the edge of the crowd. Ranks parted, making way for three men walking abreast. They wore long black coats with stars pinned on their chests. The trio came on without pause, expecting others to step aside. Which they did, without a murmur.

Olcott spat, sour-faced. He said, "Speak of the devil . . ."

LaRue said, "I'll handle them. Get going."

Olcott moved away. The trio came forward. Boyd knew them. Not personally, but he had seen them in action. The Hulls: Oates, Porter, and Courtney. Badge-wearing brothers.

Oates, the oldest, was burly, with protuberant eyes and a bushy brown mustache. The politician of the family. Porter, the middle brother, was tall, handsome, athletic. He was the enforcer, a deadly gun. Courtney, twenty-five, was the youngest. He'd killed men, but he was still raw, an unknown quantity.

Sandiford said in an aside to Boyd, "Plenty of law in Smoke Tree!"

"Too much maybe," Boyd said.

LaRue was sheriff, an elective office. Oates Hull was a U.S. marshal, federally appointed. His brothers' badges marked them as "Specials," deputies in all but name.

Oates said, "What's all the fuss?"

While Tipton told him what happened, Doc Grinnell showed up. He had gray hair and a white goatee and carried a medical bag. He climbed into the coach to examine Meg Kerner.

Porter Hull's eyes were always in motion, watchful. He eyed Boyd. Boyd lit up a thin black Mexican cigarillo and blew smoke. Porter's gaze moved on, falling on Clarissa. Their eyes met. Sparks flew. They both looked away.

A sneer was never far from Courtney's smooth, chiseled face, and it was there when Tipton finished talking.

Courtney said, "No mystery about who did it: Jeff Parry and his crowd!"

"You don't know that," LaRue said mildly.

"Parry's gang is behind most of the crime in these parts! That crowd should have been cleaned up on a long time ago!"

"You know where to find them?" LaRue asked.

"Somebody's got to protect the people of this county from being robbed and murdered!"

LaRue chuckled. "Sounds like you're running for office. I thought your big brother was the politician in the family."

"You'll know he is come November, when he takes your job."

"We'll see. Till then, I'm the sheriff. Show me some evidence that Parry's broken the law, and I'll arrest him," LaRue said. He rubbed his hands in a brisk businesslike manner. "I can't stand around here speechifying. I've got a job to do."

Courtney opened his mouth to reply, but Porter spoke first.

"Get the horses, Court," he said.

Courtney didn't want to let it go, but Porter was insistent. "Do it," Porter said.

Courtney favored LaRue with a final sneer before turning on his heel and walking away. He hadn't gotten more than a half-dozen paces before LaRue called to him:

"Hey, Courtney! Where's your pal Kip?"

Courtney stiffened, started to turn. Porter said, "The horses, Court."

Courtney shivered like a dog throwing off water, then kept on going. LaRue was grinning.

Porter said, "Best not go baiting my brother, Wade. He's got a short fuse."

"That's a bad thing for a lawman to have, Porter. Anyhow, I was surprised. It's rare to see you boys without Kip Kingston."

"Kip's a friend."

"Dangerous friend," LaRue said.

Porter shrugged, turning his attention elsewhere. It fell on Boyd. Porter's eyes narrowed, studying him.

"I know you," he said.

Boyd said, "Could be. I was in Bender when you were keeping the peace there."

"Um," Porter said. He looked like he didn't care to be reminded of his tenure as town marshal in Bender, Kansas.

A wagon came up East Mercado Street, halting at the crossroads. In it were four men: Doug Seaton, Hardrock Riley, and two guards. Seaton was manager of the Knob Knoll copper mine. His foreman, Riley, was a bald giant with a handlebar mustache. He looked like a circus strongman. The guards were miners with guns. All four, plus the horses and wagon, bore a thin coating of red dust.

Seaton, forty, looked feverish. He said, "What happened? A holdup? Good God!"

Tipton said, "They killed Butch Randle, Mr. Seaton!"

Seaton groaned.

"But they didn't get the gold!" Tipton said cheerfully.

Seaton sagged, stricken. He clutched Riley's brawny arm for support.

LaRue said, "You okay, Seaton?"

Seaton, recovering, mopped his brow with a handkerchief. "I'm all right," he said. "Thank God the payroll is safe!"

Riley said, "Amen to that."

Seaton said, "The robbers—who were they?"

Nobody knew, or if they did, they weren't saying. LaRue said, "We'll find out when we catch them. Then they'll hang."

Porter said, "We won't catch them standing around here jawing."

"My sentiments exactly," LaRue said.

Olcott returned with a nucleus of a posse—five men, all part of LaRue's crowd. They looked tough enough. They were well-armed and on horseback. They were supplied with food, water, and ammunition.

They waited while LaRue said his good-byes to Clarissa Bane. Doc Grinnell climbed down from the coach. LaRue said, "How's the patient, Doc?"

"Asthma attack," Grinnell said.

"You sound disappointed it wasn't something worse."

"I wish it was, to have called me out of a poker game when I had a winning hand!"

"Take good care of her."

"I'd rather take care of that enchanting creature on your arm, LaRue."

LaRue wagged his finger. "Mind your manners, Doc. She's my fiancée. Doc Grinnell—Clarissa Bane."

She offered her hand, and Grinnell kissed it. It was

done in a courtly manner that gave no offense.

"Charmed," he said.

Olcott held the reins of LaRue's horse. LaRue mounted up.

Oates Hull, fidgeting, said, "Where's Court?"

"Here he comes," Porter said.

Courtney rode up with three men and a string of three extra horses. Porter said, "Kip's with him."

"For once, I'm glad to see him," Oates said.

They spoke with their heads together, low-voiced— but Boyd had good ears. Porter said sharply, "Kip's a friend, brother. He saved my life."

"I know. He never lets me forget it," Oates said.

Boyd drew on his cigarillo, its glowing tip underlighting his face. Porter saw it, nudged Oates. They fell silent.

Kip Kingston looked something like Oates, big and bearish. He had thick black brows and a thick black mustache. His paunch hung over a well-worn gunbelt worn low. He was dusty, as if he'd done some hard riding, but his horse was fresh, its hide sleek.

Porter said, "I'd just about given you up for lost."

Kingston laughed. "You can't get rid of me that easily, hoss."

Two of the extra horses were saddled; the third was laden with supplies. Porter and Oates got on their horses.

LaRue said, "Best get that cashbox squared away as soon as you can, Seaton."

"I'm going to lock it in the company vault right now," Seaton said.

The posse was ready to go. Boyd said, "Hey!"

They all looked at him. He said, "I lost my hat out

there. If you find it, I'd like to have it back.''

LaRue said, ''Come along yourself, if you like. We could use another man.''

Boyd shook his head. ''No, thanks. I've had enough excitement for one day.''

The posse rode out, going north toward the pass. A townsman said, ''They'd save time if they went straight to Rock House.''

Other townsmen agreed.

Tipton said, ''Huh! If Jeff Parry had jumped us, we wouldn't be here now! When he jumps you, you stay jumped!''

The cowboys agreed with that. ''Damn right,'' one said.

Seaton said, ''Let's get that strongbox in the vault.''

His men loaded the strongbox into the wagon. It was heavy. Seaton tried the padlock, rattling it. It was intact, untouched.

Seaton and crew got in the wagon and drove away, escorted by a contingent of miners on foot. The crowd broke up, drifting away. Boyd got his gear from the stagecoach's back boot.

Sandiford said, ''Join me in a drink?''

Boyd said, ''Some other time, thanks.''

He hefted his bag and case. A local pointed out the Majestic Hotel, on the northwest corner of Grand and Mercado. Boyd went to it.

A light flickered at the far end of East Mercado Street, in the darkness outside of town: the fiery glow of the smelter at the mine. It underlit the smoke pouring from the stack and turned the moon orange. A grimy haze hung over the town. Boyd could smell it in the air.

The Majestic Hotel was three stories tall with a white-columned front. Boyd climbed the stairs, crossed the verandah, and entered the lobby. It was dimly lit. On the right was the front desk. To the left was a sitting area with a handful of armchairs, some drum tables with lamps on them, a threadbare carpet, and some potted plants. A couple of old men in cowboy hats and suits sat in the chairs, reading newspapers. Behind the sitting area was a dining room.

Clarissa Bane had just finished registering and was now climbing the stairs to the second floor, preceded by a porter who was carrying her bags. It was a pleasure watching her ripe, round rump in motion under her dress as she went upstairs.

Weaver, the desk clerk, had a high shiny forehead, arched eyebrows, and wide side-whiskers. Boyd set down his gear and signed the register. He signed it *Frank Bowman*.

Weaver said, "The boy will show you to your room."

The "boy" turned out to be a wizened sixty-five-year-old man. He was stooped, with jughandle ears. He tried to lift Boyd's long case and nearly ruined himself. It barely budged. Boyd picked it up and held it under one arm. The porter carried his bag. Boyd could have carried that too, but he figured the porter might as well earn his keep.

The room was on the third floor's southeast corner. It had a good view of the town crossroads. That was why he had taken it. The porter unlocked the door, set down the bag, and lit a table lamp. There was a bed, night table, standing wardrobe, writing table, chair, and a chest of drawers. On top of the chest of drawers was a wash basin and a mirror.

Boyd tipped the porter and he went away. The room was stuffy. Boyd opened the windows. The panes were dirty and there was grime on the sills. Breezes lifted the curtains. He stuck his head outside. There was no balcony. Ten feet below the bottom of the window was the second-floor balcony, which bordered three sides of the building.

Boyd's stomach rumbled. He went downstairs in search of something to eat. The dining room was still open. No partition separated it from the rest of the lobby.

A black-haired woman in a shiny green dress crossed to him. She was about thirty, exotic-looking, with Spanish blood. Her hair was parted in the middle, pulled down tight along the sides of her head, and gathered in a knot at the back of her neck. She had wide dark almond-shaped eyes, amber skin, and sharp cheekbones. Her harsh, almost predatory good looks were offset by a wide-lipped, sensual red mouth. Black onyx stones set in gold buttons were pinned to her earlobes—the only jewelry she wore.

Boyd asked if he could get something to eat. She said yes. A man and a woman sat at a table on the left side of the room, finishing their meals. Silverware rattled against plates. Boyd sat on the right side of the room, back to the wall, where he could see who came and went. Nobody came in. The couple finished their meal and left. The woman in green brought Boyd's order: steak, potatoes, and salad greens, then black coffee and dessert, blueberry pie.

Boyd said, "Good pie. Believe I'll have me some more."

The woman in green said, "You ate the last piece."

"Well, that was good pie."

He settled up and went out to the front porch for a smoke. A group of loafers had congregated there. They didn't look like they were staying at the hotel. They jawed over the night's events. Boyd listened. He learned that LaRue and Oates Hull didn't like each other; that LaRue and Porter Hull liked each other less; that Courtney Hull was a loudmouth, Kip Kingston was a killer, and Jeff Parry was a bad hombre. Nothing he didn't already know.

He finished his smoke and ground out the stub under his heel. He was about to go in when he heard somebody say, "Kingston sure rode into town tonight like a bat out of hell."

Another loafer said innocently, "When was that, Avery?"

"Right before the stagecoach pulled in!"

"So?"

"So? Why you damned fool, what do you think he was doing out there right about the time the stagecoach was jumped?!"

"You mean—?"

"It wouldn't be the first time Kingston's played road agent," Avery said.

A third member of the group was white-bearded and scrawny-necked. He stiffened, said, "I ain't heard nothing," and walked away.

Avery said, "Huh! What's wrong with him?" He was red-faced, slack-jawed with drink.

A fourth man said, "You're the damned fool, Avery. Kingston's got a lot of friends in this town."

Avery was sobering, worried. He said, "I was just talking, Dutch, I didn't mean nothing."

"You'll talk yourself to death," Dutch said. He made a shooing gesture. "Get going, Avery. I don't want to be around you when the shooting starts."

Avery yelped. "Shooting? Who says there's gonna be any shooting? Quit funning, Dutch."

Dutch clenched a big fist. "I ain't funning. Get the hell out of here."

The loafer who'd been chatting with Avery said, "Hit him, Dutch!"

Avery sidled away. Dutch laughed and said, "He ain't worth it."

Avery slunk across the porch and down the stairs. He looked both ways, up and down Mercado Street. He went west, away from the lights. His head was down and he walked bent forward, as if fighting a heavy wind. He kept glancing back over his shoulder. The fear was in him.

Boyd lit a fresh cigarillo, but the loafers were through talking freely in the presence of strangers. He finished his smoke and went up to his room.

He made sure that the window curtains were closed before lighting the lamp. That made it tougher for snipers. He hung up his jacket, opened his shirt, and rolled up his sleeves. From his bag, he took a bottle of whiskey and set it aside. He set his long case down on the bed and unlocked it, opening it.

It was a gun case. The interior was lined with velvet. It held a long rifle, a six-foot-long custom-made piece with an octagonal barrel. Boyd had made it himself. He was a skilled gunsmith. The long gun was caliber .70. Big .70.

Also in the case were a scope, a bipod, and ammunition.

Boyd took out the long gun and examined it. It had survived the trip none the worse for wear. He'd expected no less. The weapon was spotless, but he ran a cleaning cloth over it. The scope, more delicate, required greater scrutiny. It didn't take much to throw the precisely machined telescopic sight out of line. It was flukey. But the .70 rifle could shoot so far and true that sometimes a scope was a good thing to have. The scope passed visual inspection, but firing it would tell the tale.

He closed the case and put it away. On the bed table was a tray with a pitcher of water and two glasses. He filled one glass with water, left the other empty, and set them both down on the writing desk. He put his two sixguns on the desk. Then a gun-cleaning kit. He filled the empty glass with whiskey. Whiskey could be a problem. Sometimes he liked it too much. He had a reason for getting drunk, but what drunk didn't? So he didn't get drunk anymore. He drank, though.

He swallowed some whiskey, shuddered, and sipped some water. He sat, turning his chair so he faced the locked door. Habit. He cleaned one gun. The other lay on its side, loaded, within reach. From time to time, he drank whiskey and water. When the gun was clean, he placed it on the desktop near his fingertips, unloaded the other gun, and began cleaning that one. He drank whiskey and water.

Task done, he put the guns aside and drank whiskey

and water. He took some maps out of his bag. He took off his shirt and boots, stretched out on the bed, and spread open the maps. They were copies of relief maps of the area drawn by army surveyors. Boyd studied them, sipping whiskey.

When he was done, he swept the maps off the bed with his arm, knocking them to the floor. He'd pick them up tomorrow. He stripped, put out the lights, and crawled between the sheets, a gun in his hand. He slept with the gun beside him. Handy, in case of trouble.

He was sore from the long stagecoach trip. He fell asleep, dreaming that he was still riding in the coach.

He awoke. He was sitting up in bed, gun raised, heart pounding. Light flashed through the windows from outside. A thunderclap sounded, shaking the walls.

A storm. No, not a storm. More flashes, more blasts. He went to the window. It was late. The town was dark. Knob Knoll was alight. The mine site looked like a volcano that had blown its top. Yellow-white flares underlit mountains of smoke. Blast echoes rumbled, fading away.

There was a stunned silence. Dogs began to bark all over town. Lights came on, windows were opened, heads thrust outside. A rider galloped through the crossroads toward the knoll. People stepped into the street, barefoot, rubbing their eyes. They ran to and fro. The night was filled with alarms and commotions.

Boyd poured a drink and sat at the window in the dark room, watching the show. A man in the street shouted, "They've blown the safe at the mine!"

It looked like they'd blown the mine off the knoll.

Pieces of flaming wreckage rained down, some starting fires where they fell.

When the clamor finally died, Boyd went back to bed. He needed sleep. Tomorrow would be a big day.

Two

Knob Knoll was a quarter mile east of town. The knob was a big bald rock, tall as a church steeple. It looked like a brooding fetus, big-headed and small-bodied. A road went up the knoll and around the rock. Beyond lay a flat, an eighth of a mile long and a few hundred yards wide. Beyond that, a rocky ridge. Centered on the flat, near the ridge, were the mine's aboveground works. Ore crusher, separator, and smelter, each housed in its own barnlike shed, all tied together by a gridded framework of platforms, scaffolds, conveyer belts. Narrow-gauged rails for ore carts tracked back to gaping tunnel mouths in the ridge face.

Mills and machines were silent. The furnace was cold, the chimney smokeless. Near the works, but apart from them, had stood the administrative building. In it had been the company offices, records, and a bank-type vault. The site was now occupied by a smoking crater.

It must have been some blast. The building was pulverized, not a wall left standing. It had been chewed to bits and the pieces spat out all across the flat. The crater was three feet deep at its center and as big across as a large saloon. It was dark reddish-brown, contrasting with the sandy topsoil. Chunks of stone and lumps of fused metal, remnants of the vault, littered the scene. Other buildings had sustained blast damage, idling the machinery.

The miners were idle too. A crowd of them massed on the grounds, surly, stunned, silent. They shuffled around in the debris, hands in pockets, faces set. Seaton stood on a wagon, trying to talk them into going back to work.

Apart from the miners was a second, smaller group: the curious. Among them was Boyd. He was bareheaded. A gun was tucked into his waistband, jacket buttoned over it. He had walked from town.

It was light, before sunup. Red dust hung in the air, fine as mist. It was always there, a byproduct of the copper mine, but stirred up thicker than usual by the blast. Dew damped down some of the dust, not enough. It was going to be a hot day. It was already hot.

Boyd walked around the crater. Over to the side, Seaton still harangued the miners, urging them back to work. They weren't buying, but at least they weren't throwing rocks. Seaton's man, Riley, was nowhere to be seen, but other guards were nearby, unobtrusive, watchful.

Most of the town lawmen were out on the trail, chasing the unsuccessful stagecoach robbers. Left behind by the sheriff, and now watching at the mine, was Senior Deputy Mal Joslyn. Senior in years, not in rank. He was heavy, dour. With him were two cowboys he'd deputized but lacked badges for. Representing the Hull faction was Tom Krang, bartender at Jack Grand's Beacon Saloon, a Hull stronghold. He wore a derby and smoked a cigar. No jacket, a vest, a shirt with sleeve garters, a pistol stuck in his pants, and no badge. A few drunks hung in his wake, hoping to promote a free drink later—a forlorn hope.

Joslyn, the two cowboys, Tom Krang, the drunks, and a few dozen assorted spectators watched a red-haired man poke around the blast site. The redhead was slight, pale, freckled, with quick skittish movements.

Boyd said, "Who's that?"

"Pete Hooper," said a man nearby. "Dynamiter for the mine."

"Seems a mite high-strung," Boyd said.

"That job would make anyone high-strung!"

The man spoke low-voiced, as if afraid of disturbing Hooper, now well out of earshot. He said, "He must be good—he's got all his fingers!"

Hooper paced off distances at intervals around the crater, jotting them down on a notepad. He inspected debris. He picked up a piece of fused metal, peering at it through wire-rimmed lenses. He discarded it, picked up another piece, put it in an envelope, sealed it, marked some notations on the outside, and pocketed it.

He entered the crater, scuttling around on its floor. He walked bent forward, his upper body almost parallel to the ground. He circled the inner rim, spiraling toward its center. He paused frequently, at ever-longer intervals, taking samples and making notes. A few times, he sniffed the air, seeking some elusive trace. To Boyd, the site stank of cordite, rock dust, and burning.

At one point, Hooper, struck by some detail known only to himself, struck a thoughtful pose and said, "Hmmm." Immediately thereafter, he resumed his routine.

Deputy Joslyn nodded a few times, looking wise, pretending he knew what the hell it was all about.

Seaton, hoarse, was winding up his argument to the miners. He said: "The owners will pay off on a working mine a damned sight quicker than they will on an idle one!"

The miners stayed put. Seaton got down from the wagon.

A delegation of town dignitaries was arriving. Seaton went to meet them. The miners followed. Seaton's guards didn't like the miners pressing so close to their man, but there was nothing they could do about it but tag along.

The mayor of Smoke Tree was Clarence Millet. The town banker was Bailey Daigle. The *Gazette*, the town paper, was owned by Phin Conway. Millet, Daigle, Conway; mayor, banker, publisher. Millet was gray-haired, deep-chested. Daigle was shrewd, sharp-faced. Conway was jowly, with a bulbous nose.

To the mine, before dawn, they came, trailed by an

entourage of flunkies and hangers-on. They were met by Seaton. Hooper climbed out of the crater to join them. At the fringes, where they could hear what was being said, the miners massed.

The mayor threw his arms up into the air, sputtering, "It's a damned outrage!"

"Right before an election too," Conway said, with mock sympathy.

The mayor glared but let it pass, not so confident of the *Gazette*'s backing as to needlessly antagonize its publisher.

Seaton eyed the banker evenly. He said, "Come to gloat, Daigle?"

Daigle shook his head. "It pains me to see the destruction of so much capital. What a waste." He sounded sad. "You kept your money here, Seaton, in your own vault, because you thought it was safer than the bank's. Ironic, isn't it?"

"Yes—very. Too bad I didn't take your advice. Then it'd be your bank in ruins."

"We'll never know," Daigle said cheerfully.

"You will if this lawlessness keeps up," Millet said.

Daigle frowned. "That's hardly encouraging, Mayor. After all, we look to you for leadership in protecting the public."

"The public trough, you mean," Conway said.

Millet colored. "Enough of your insults, Conway, unless you want a thrashing!"

He shook his fist at the publisher. Conway paled, stepping back.

"Here, now!" Conway said.

Daigle said, "Keep that up, Millet, and I may vote for you myself!"

Millet looked as if he wouldn't mind tangling with Daigle too, but he kept silent.

In the lull, Joslyn said, "It was your dynamite did the blasting, Seaton." Not accusing, just stating a fact.

"Ironic, isn't it?" Seaton said, echoing Daigle, mimicking the banker's dry tone and delivery.

Seaton went on. "The thieves broke into a shed and stole some explosives. They used them to blow up the vault."

"They were a mite over-enthusiastic," one of the cowboy deputies said.

Seaton said, "They used too much. Blew up the vault and everything in it, blew it to atoms."

The cowboy deputy made a face. "You mean all that beautiful gold's been blasted into the sweet by-and-by?"

Seaton nodded. "Some powder and fragments were mixed in with the wreckage, but they were picked clean by the crowd."

Conway said, "You're the explosives expert, Hooper. That how you see it?"

Hooper said, "The shed was broken into. That was our dynamite."

Joslyn said, "Kinda careless of you to leave it where anybody could pick it up and use it."

Seaton said, "There was a guard. Craigie, Joe Craigie."

"Craigie, eh? I want to talk to him," Joslyn said.

"You can't. He's gone."

"Where to?"

"I don't know. Nobody does. He's vanished. He was last seen while on duty last night, before the blast."

"I don't like the sound of this, Seaton." Joslyn's expression indicated that he liked the sound of this very much. "This looks like an inside job to me!"

A cowboy deputy said, "Reckon this Craigie's in on it, Mal?"

"Could be," Joslyn said.

"Nonsense," Hooper said. "I knew Craigie. He was honest, dependable."

"Mebbe so, mebbe so," Joslyn said. He pushed his hat brim higher up on his forehead. His eyes were bloodshot, baggy, their turquoise irises filmed over. Tobacco stains discolored his ragged mustache ends. Liquor was on his breath.

But he wore a badge. So he said, "Where were you last night, Hooper?"

Hooper laughed, a sharp piping like a birdcall. He said, "If I wanted to open the vault, I'd have done a neater job than that!"

"Which don't exactly answer the question," Joslyn said.

"I was in bed, asleep," Hooper said. "Alone, if that's any of your business."

"It's the law's business. I notice you spoke of Craigie in the past tense. You *knew* him, you said. He *was* honest."

"I spoke that way because it is my firm conviction that Joe Craigie is, in fact, dead!"

"Why?"

"I told you why. Craigie was honest, not the type to get involved with desperadoes," Hooper said.

"He was a good man," Seaton said.

Joslyn said, "People are funny critters. You never know when one of them's going to up and jump the fence."

Hooper said, "I believe that Craigie saw too much and was killed for his troubles."

"Can you prove it?" Joslyn said.

Hooper shook his head, irritated. "No, of course not."

"There you are. If they killed him, where's the body?"

"Lots of places to hide a body around the mine."

"If it's hid, we'll find it," Joslyn said.

Seaton said, "Maybe not."

Joslyn turned toward him, hands on hips. "Why not?"

"He might have been blown up with the building. You saw what that blast did to steel and stone. Pulverized it. Flesh and blood wouldn't stand a chance against it," Seaton said.

"The same might have happened to the thieves. If they were caught in the blast, we couldn't find them with a fine-toothed comb," he added.

Conway said, "Thieves killed by their own bomb? Neat, but a bit too pat. My readers won't like that."

Seaton said, "I don't give a hang for your readers, Conway."

"May I quote you?"

"Quote and be damned!"

Joslyn said, "You're forgetting something, Seaton. The thieves' horses."

"What about them?"

"There weren't any. The thieves must have rode out on them."

Seaton weighed this, conceding. "It was only a theory."

Joslyn nodded, satisfied, as if he had taken a point in a game.

Seaton said, "We acted on the assumption that the gang had indeed gotten away. Whatever tracks they made were destroyed by the crowd that swarmed the site last night. Riley is leading a search party to try to cut their trail. But they're miners, not manhunters. We need professionals."

Tom Krang spoke for the first time. "Why don't you get after them, Joslyn?"

"And leave Smoke Tree defenseless, in case somebody tries to rob Mr. Daigle's bank, say, or shoot up the town? Can't do that, Krang."

"I'll look after things while you're away."

"Your duties are liable to keep you chained pretty close to the bar, Krang. I'll stay," Joslyn said.

Millet said, "Where's LaRue when we need him?"

"Chasing them stagecoach robbers, Mayor," Joslyn said.

"It's an outrage, a damned outrage!" Millet shouted. "We're besieged by banditry!" Spittle flew from Millet's mouth.

The others stepped back, out of the way. Krang cocked an ear in the direction of town, saying, "I hear my duties calling me back to the bar."

The drunks laughed it up. One slapped Krang on the back, saying, "You said a mouthful, Tom!"

"I'll drink a gutful. This peacekeeping is thirsty work," Krang said.

The drunks whooped it up even more. Krang studied the backslapper, his eyes narrow.

He said, "Keep your hands off of me, less'n you want your arms torn off."

The drunk reeled, stricken. Krang thrust his face forward and said, "Boo!"

The backslapper tripped over his own feet and sat down hard in the mud. Krang slapped his knee and said, "Haw!"

The other drunks roared. The butt of their mirth managed to muster up a sickly smile.

Boyd stood apart, unmoved. Conway came alongside him, saying, "Mr. Bowman?"

Boyd said, "What can I do for you?"

"I'm Conway, the manager, editor, and sometime scribe for the *Gazette,* the town paper."

"That's how you knew my name, huh?"

"You're news. A hero."

"The scaredest one you ever saw."

"You're too modest. It took a brave man to shoot it out with those outlaws."

"If I hit anything, it was a miracle."

"Do you think the robbers were the same bunch who struck here?"

Boyd shrugged. "Who knows? The one you want to talk to is Sandiford."

"The other man in the coach."

"He's the real hero. He opened up on those robbers. I just followed his lead."

"I've met the man," Conway said. "Staying in town long, Mr. Bowman?"

"Depends."

"What brings you to Smoke Tree?"

"Business."

Conway caught the subtle change in Boyd's tone. "Hope you don't mind all these questions. That's my job."

"I can stand it. You going to put this in your newspaper?"

"Maybe. It never hurts to have some background on visitors to our town."

"How come you're not writing anything down?"

Conway tapped the side of his head. "It's all in here. I'll write it later. What business are you in, Mr. Bowman?"

"Livestock futures."

"Buying or selling?"

"Depends on the price," Boyd said.

"You came to the right place. There's cattle ranching throughout the Sinagua. A speculator could do well here."

"That's me," Boyd said. "A speculator."

"Good luck," Conway said.

The crowd of spectators was breaking up, drifting back toward town. Boyd went with them.

The sun rose, spiking Boyd's shadow a hundred yards before him. Long, spidery, gigantic, it slid across the landscape. The illusion tickled him. "I'm a giant," he thought. He noticed that all the people on the knoll

cast similar shadows. That took some of the fun
away. The shadows looked like a column of black
snakes descending on the town.

The sun was hot on Boyd's head and the back of
his neck. Its first rays burnt off the dew. Boyd sorely
missed his hat.

The town was astir. The whores were going to
bed—to sleep, that is—while the decent folk, so-
called, were up and doing. There was movement in
the street, people, horses. Two workmen loaded boxes
into a wagon. A shop's boy swept out the front of a
store. Beneath his feet, under the plank sidewalk, a
cat crouched, its green eyes ablaze in darkness.

A passerby pointed out the Wells Fargo office to
Boyd, on the north side of Mercado, west of Grand.
It was closed.

Boyd said, "Can you beat that? Banker's hours!"

Returning to the hotel, he had the sun in his face.
It was sharp, blinding. He squinted, eyes almost
closed. By comparison, the lobby was a cool twilight
grotto. Pink and yellow afterimages floated before his
eyes. He stood to one side until they went away. He
went into the dining room. It was crowded, with most
of the tables taken. He found one that wasn't and sat
down. His temples throbbed. Too much sun on his
bare head. His hangover might have had something to
do with it too.

A girl came to take his order. She was young, in
her teens. Straight blond hair was pinned to the top
of her head, out of the way. She had an adult face,
finely featured, with bright blue eyes and sulky pink
mouth. She wore a blue-and-white checked gingham

dress. She was willowy, with enough curves to make it interesting.

Boyd said, "Where's that woman in a bright green dress, minds the dining room at night?"

"Miss Delores, you mean," the girl said.

"Good-looking black-haired woman."

"That's her. She won't be here till mid-morning. Likes to sleep late." The girl gave Boyd a veiled glance, which could have meant a lot of things.

She said, "Why her, mister? Won't I do?"

"Do what?"

"What have you got in mind?"

"Right now, breakfast," Boyd said. "What's your name, pretty girl?"

"Holly. What's yours?"

"Frank."

She stood where he could get a good look at her. "Hungry, Frank?"

"Starved. So let's have that grub."

He wolfed a big plateful of steak and eggs and fries, and drank a quart of black coffee. A man at a nearby table was eating sweet rolls. Boyd said, "Are they fresh?"

"Baked this morning," Holly said.

He had sweet rolls for dessert, washed down with more coffee. He settled up the bill and went out to the verandah for a smoke. A new crop of loafers monopolized the chairs. He stood leaning against a pillar and lit up. The smoke was hot, harsh. So was the daylight.

He went to his room. Sunlight shafted through the east window, filtered through rising dust. Red dust filmed the windowsill. It settled on the furniture and floor. Boyd pulled down the shade, closing the light. There was still enough to see by.

He opened the gun case. A thing of beauty, the long rifle was precisely tooled, lovingly tended. Like a Sioux lance or a samurai sword, it hummed with lethal potential.

His fingertips brushed the barrel, leaving marks. He used a cloth to wipe them off. Regretfully he closed the lid and set aside the gun case. The Time of the Big .70 was yet to come.

He changed to range clothes: short brown jacket, gray shirt, brown pants. In the jacket pockets was a pair of gloves. He put on his gunbelt. He had two guns but only one holster. What to do with the extra? He debated leaving it behind, but decided to take it, stuffing it butt-out in his pants over his left hip. The jacket covered it, mostly. An extra gun was always good.

He fitted the folded maps in an inside breast pocket. He picked up the gun case and started out the door. Midway through it, he reflexively started back for his hat, then remembered that he didn't have one.

"Man needs a hat," he said.

He locked the room door and went downstairs. Weaver was manning the front desk. Boyd said he wanted to check his gun case for safekeeping. Weaver got someone to mind the desk, and led Boyd through a narrow door at the far end of the counter. Beyond lay a passage, its low ceiling the underside of a slanted staircase. It smelled of wood. The passage met a hallway at right angles. The hall was long, high,

narrow. The right-hand branch ended in a wall. Set
high up in it was a thin vertical window. At the end
of the left-hand branch was an outside door, chained
and bolted.

Opposite the passage, across the hall, was a wall in
which stood a door, ironbound and padlocked. Weaver deftly selected a key from his crowded key ring,
fitted it into the padlock, and opened it. The door
opened on a small windowless storeroom, not much
bigger than a walk-in pantry. The air was thick,
musty. A central aisle reached to the far wall. On either side, storage shelves reached to the ceiling. The
lower shelves held dust-furred suitcases with tags, hotel bric-a-brac, and other clutter, mostly junk.

Boyd followed Weaver into the room. It was
murky with brown shadows. Dust itched Boyd's nose.
On a shelf to the right of the door was a half-melted
candle stuck to a saucer. Weaver lit it, filling the
room with a rich bronze glow. He went to the end of
the aisle, making more room for Boyd. He set the
candle-and-saucer down on top of an upended steamer
trunk.

Boyd said, "You get a lot of folks trying to skip
out on the bill?"

"Oh, you must mean the luggage," Weaver said.
"There's always a few bad apples, but that's not really the problem. You can make money in Smoke
Tree, but you can lose it too. Sometimes a guest finds
himself financially overextended. When that happens,
we secure their personal property here for safekeeping
until they can make restitution."

Boyd cleared a space on a shoulder-high shelf to

his left. He said, "Okay if I set it here?"

"Anywhere," Weaver said.

Boyd set the case flat on the shelf. Weaver said, "I'll have to verify the contents. Hotel policy, I'm afraid."

Boyd nodded. "Don't want anybody sticking you with a pig in a poke."

"Not my policy, hotel policy."

"I don't blame you. There's a lot of slippery cusses around," Boyd said.

He opened the case and raised the lid. Candlelight gleamed on the long rifle's burnished metal surfaces, highlighting them with molten gold. Weaver made an involuntary exclamation of surprise. He moved closer, intrigued.

He said, "My, that is a beauty! What an unusual rifle . . . I don't believe I've ever seen one quite like that. What is it, a buffalo gun?"

"Something like," Boyd said. But a buffalo gun was .50-caliber, and this was a big .70.

"No more buffalo now," Weaver said, "not that there ever were any in these parts. A hunter, are you, Mr. Bowman?"

"That's my passion. If things work out, I just might take off to the hills for a few days, in search of some game.

"Business permitting," he added with a thin smile.

"I'm a big booster of Smoke Tree, Mr. Bowman, but I'd be remiss in my duties if I didn't point out that this can be dangerous country for a man alone. There are some desperate characters out there."

"So I've noticed. Thanks for the warning," Boyd said. "Seen enough?"

"Yes."

Boyd closed the case and locked it. Without the rifle as a reflector, the candlelight dimmed. The flame flickered as Weaver moved the candle closer to the case. He put a tag on the case, and tore off the bottom half and gave it to Boyd. Boyd went into the hall. Weaver paused at the door, blew out the candle, and put it back where he had found it.

He sealed up the room, locking it from the outside. When he was done, he saw that Boyd was holding up a gold coin. It glimmered, struck by a sunbeam slanting down from the high window.

Boyd gave him the coin, saying, "Thanks."

"Thank you." Then Weaver saw the size of the coin. "And thanks again."

"That's a valuable piece of equipment in there. I know you'll take good care of it."

"I'd have done that in any case, Mr. Bowman. But it's nice to be appreciated. All such tokens are gratefully accepted. I can use it. I'm a hired man, you know, not the owner."

"Sometimes the hunting urge hits me all at once. No matter what time it is, day or night, there's nothing for it but for me to get on the trail after some game. What I'm saying is, I might want to lay my hand on that piece at some mighty short notice."

"There's always someone at the desk. When you want your property, just present your half of the ticket. I'll instruct the others to take care of you immediately."

"Quiet-like," Boyd said. "No fuss."

It was Weaver's turn to smile thinly. "My preeminent position in this hotel is due in no small part to my discretion, sir."

"Good. I'm a man that hates fuss," Boyd said.

Weaver ducked under the stairs, making for the door to the front. Boyd said, "One more thing."

Weaver paused, looking back.

Boyd said, "Where can I get a new hat?"

The Wells Fargo office was still closed. That made Boyd hot under the collar. He was hot all over. He'd delayed getting a hat so he could try the freight office again. The town was up and doing, but not Wells Fargo. Meanwhile, the sun beat down on his head.

He rattled the doorknob, then stood on tiptoes trying to peer around the edges of the shades and into the office. It was black dark, alone, untenanted.

Two doors away was a barbershop. The barber stepped outside, emptying a basin of dirty water in the street. His hair was parted in the middle and he had a tricky, complicated little mustache. He said, "It's closed, mister."

"That right?" Boyd said. "Where's Bland?"

"Fred Bland? The Fargo man?"

"Yes."

"Yonder," the barber said, pointing west.

He indicated a rise outside of town, its slope studded with twisted crosses. A graveyard.

Boyd said, "Boot Hill? How?"

"Late Tuesday night, somebody shot him from behind. Blew his brains out."

Today was Thursday. Bland had been killed the night before the attempted stagecoach robbery.

Boyd said, "Who did it?"

The barber shrugged. "Nobody knows. Bland a friend of yours?"

"Never met the man. Had some business with the office and heard he was the agent."

"He was. He was a lot of things: notary public, town clerk, part-time assayer, Cattleman's Association representative, church elder, you name it. Damned hard man to replace."

Boyd shook his head. "Bland killed, the stagecoach attacked, the payroll robbed from the mine or maybe blown up—man, it's hard times for Wells Fargo."

"They can stand it. It's Smoke Tree I'm worried about. This violence has got to stop!"

"Um," Boyd said. "Anybody take Bland's place?"

"Cliff Olcott. Know him?"

"The deputy? I've seen him around."

"Well, he's filling in for Bland until the company decides on who they want for a permanent replacement. But he's out on a posse," the barber said.

He snickered. "Wait'll they get back! While they were off on a wild-goose chase, this town was getting blown to hell!"

"They'll probably split a gut," Boyd said. He nodded his thanks and moved on.

Occupying most of the southeast block of Grand and Mercado was Jack Grand's Store Barn Emporium. It was huge, filled with things. Boyd tried on some hats, finding them all stiff and uncomfortable.

The one he hated least, he bought. "Man needs a hat," he said.

The storklike store clerk nodded, writing up his order. Boyd wasn't through yet. He'd been in such a hurry to reach Smoke Tree that he'd had to leave most of his outfit behind. Even so, he'd arrived too late. Things were already happening.

He'd brought the tools of his trade, the six-guns and long rifle. Now he needed trail gear, supplies, and a horse. A pile of purchases grew on the floor beside the end of the counter. The gun rack yielded a carbine. Behind the back of the building was a small target range with an eight-foot-tall dirt-mound berm at the far end. Boyd steadied the carbine on a sandbag and sighted it in. The hat brim kept getting in his way. He folded it back, but it kept flopping forward. He took it off and resumed firing, head throbbing from the heat. The clerk stood nearby, watching, so Boyd made sure not to shoot too well. At this stage of the game, he didn't want word of his marksmanship to get out. For a store-bought weapon, the carbine was a nice piece. A good little saddle gun.

The clerk toted up the bill. Boyd said, "You Jack Grand?"

The clerk chuckled, not looking up from his column of figures. "Not me, brother."

"His name's plastered up all over town. He must be a big man."

"He was. Jack Grand founded this town. He was a prospector, struck a vein of silver up at Knob Knoll. A boom town sprang up overnight. He owned most of it. He was elected mayor too. Quite a character,

they say. I never met the man myself. That was before my time. He was long gone before I got here."

"What happened?"

"Silver played out. The mine went bust and the
town too. Grand lost everything and went away, nobody knows where. Town would have gone with it, if
not for the ranchers. Sinagua's prime cattle country,
mister. Kept the town going. And the mine's come
back. Not far from Grand's old diggings they found
copper, a big lode. The company's dug out tons, with
no sign of a letup."

Boyd said, "They're not digging today."

"Ain't that the darnedest thing? Glad it didn't happen to the town bank. That's where I keep my
money," the clerk said.

He finished adding the sum and showed it to Boyd.
He'd talked throughout his addition, but it proved ac-
curate down to the last cent.

Boyd paid. He said, "How come Jack Grand's
name is still up?"

The clerk said, "Why should I pay for a new sign-
board? Besides, it's what you might call historic."

Boyd left his gear at the store while he went to see
a man about a horse.

Ebberline's Corral was on the northeast block of
Liberty Street and Powell. Powell Street was east of
Grand and ran parallel to it. Boyd went north on
Powell. To his right was open ground, sloping in the
distance to Knob Knoll.

He was damned tired of walking. Liberty, the cross
street, neared. From the left came loud voices, commotion. A couple of drunk cowboys staggered out of

a saloon. It was not yet quite nine o'clock in the morning. Boyd frowned. It was getting late.

He angled across the square to Ebberline's. Stables and corral occupied the entire square block. Ebberline himself was big, slovenly, with long graying hair hanging down into his eyes. He wore a stiff brown leather vest over a bare torso, every inch of which was covered with thick reddish-brown body hair.

Boyd didn't like the looks of the horses penned in the corral, a spiritless, failing lot. Ebberline stood nearby, arms folded over his chest, resting on top of his paunch. Sly-eyed, he was all but openly sneering.

In a confidential tone, Boyd said, "Ever heard of Mark Dunston?"

"Who hasn't?" Ebberline said. "He's the biggest rancher in these parts!"

"Shh! Not so loud," Boyd said. "Dunston wouldn't like us tossing his name around out loud. He's a private man."

"That's a fact. Keeps to himself on that big spread of his."

"Suppose I told you that Dunston said you'd take good care of me."

"Well, that's different!" Ebberline rubbed his hands together. "Glad to help out any friend of Mr. Dunston's."

"That's what I thought," Boyd said.

A stable hand went to the stalls, returning with a gray gelding at the end of a halter rope. Short, stocky, strong, and surefooted, the gray was a good cow pony. Boyd approved.

Boyd and Ebberline dickered, the latter halfheartedly, going through the motions. A not-bad saddle was thrown in as part of the deal. Even Boyd had to admit (to himself) that the price was fair. Ebberline tried his manful best to hide the pain.   .

He said, "You be sure to tell Mr. Dunston I took good care of you!"

Boyd said, "I'm going to see him this afternoon."

Three

The plateau was incorporated as Sinagua County, Arizona Territory. It was big, a mile-high oval table bounded on the east by a rock-rimmed precipice and on the west by mountains. Near its center lay Smoke Tree. Slickrock Creek ran across the flat, winding from northwest to southeast. It spilled off the cliffs, continuing its journey on the ground below, eventually being swallowed up by the Verde River. The western half of the oval was prime cattle country, the Five Creeks district. In the shadow of the mountains lay well-watered grazing lands. Fat grass, good climate, with the mountains buffering the severity of winter storms. Most of the Apaches in the area had been wiped out, although every now and then a small band of wide-ranging strays would make a quick sortie, with devastating results. A lone Apache was a war party all by himself. But the threat had lessened. Rustlers and outlaws, now, they were a menace.

Biggest of all local ranchers was Mark Dunston. His

ranch, The Crossing, occupied the lion's share of the best grassland for miles on both sides of Slickrock Creek, about midway between the mountains and Smoke Tree. It took its name from a ford in the creek, a popular crossing site. It had been known as Grand's Ford, but Dunston had changed the name to The Crossing and made it stick.

Dunston had gray hair, a brown seamed face, turkey neck, and gnarled hands. His eyes were sharp, clear. He was straight-backed, stiff-necked.

He said, "Who are you and what do you want?"

Boyd said, "I told you. I'm Bowman, a cattle buyer."

"Like hell!"

They were in the study, a place in the big ranch house where Dunston conducted private business. They stood near the door, having just entered the room. Opposite them, in the far wall, a picture window let in early afternoon sunlight.

Dunston said, "I pretended to believe you outside, in front of the others, to keep foolish tongues from wagging. But you're no buyer. I know all the big buyers in the territory, and their agents, and you're not one of them. Hell, you don't even look like a buyer."

"What do I look like then?"

"Trouble. That's what you look like to me, Bowman: trouble. Maybe for somebody else, maybe for yourself, if I don't like what you have to say. Either way, it's trouble, and that's something I don't need any more of. Now, say your piece and be quick about it. And it better be good, or I'll boot you out myself!"

Boyd went deeper into the room, crossing a Navaho

carpet. Dunston followed, saying, "Where do you think you're going?!"

Fun was fun, but Boyd had had enough. He turned, facing Dunston, hands on hips.

He said, "Some talk is best kept private. What I have to say is for you alone, Dunston."

Dunston was brought up short. He looked surprised, then crafty. He said guardedly, "You're Mayfield?"

That gave Boyd a start, though he didn't show it. *Dale Mayfield!* Things must have come to a pretty pass for Dunston to have called in a hired gun like Mayfield.

That complicates things, he thought.

He said, "I'm not Mayfield."

Disappointment showed on Dunston's face, followed by swift-mounting rage. Before he could go off, Boyd spoke first.

"I'm from the Cattleman's Protective Association," Boyd said.

Dunston, thrown, had to think this through. Finally he said, "Where the hell have you been?!"

"I'm here now," Boyd said.

When he'd first gotten word of the mission, he'd traveled light, leaving behind his horse and saddle in the interest of speed, planning to replace them when he reached his destination. He'd crossed hundreds of miles nonstop by train and stagecoach, arriving in quick time. He mentioned none of this to Dunston, because he knew Dunston wouldn't give a damn.

Dunston, impassioned, said, "I was the first in Sinagua to join the Association! I'm a longtime dues-paying member in good standing. What's the Association done for me, now that I need them? Nothing!"

"What about Fred Bland? He do enough for you? He's dead."

"That's none of my doing," Dunston said. "The man was a disgrace, no better than a crook. Nobody knows how many irons he had in the fire. If you want to find his killer—you do, don't you, him being a fellow Association man?—my advice is, look in Smoke Tree."

"That's your advice, huh? Smoke Tree is part of the problem. What happens in town affects the county, and vice versa."

"True. But so what? That's just talk. What can you do, one lone man?"

"Mayfield's a lone wolf too," Boyd said.

Dunston paced over to his desk, putting it between himself and Boyd. He leaned forward, hands on the desktop. He was edgy, evasive.

"Never mind about Mayfield," he said.

"You sent for him."

Dunston raised a hand, palm-up. "That's none of your business."

"Wrong. It is my business. I've got a job to do and I don't want gunmen like Mayfield getting in the way."

"What job?" Dunston said, sneering but interested.

Boyd said, "Troubleshooter. When I find trouble, I shoot it."

"Big talk," Dunston sneered, almost happy. He sat down, sinking into the chair behind his desk.

Boyd said, "The Association takes its duties seriously. You're not the only member in Five Creeks whose rights need protecting, Dunston."

"I'm the biggest, so protect me best. Hell, who do you think the rustlers steal from? The man with the big-

gest herds: me. They come out of the mountain passes,
cut out as many head as they can, and run them back
into the mountains. Anyone who follows, they kill!''

"Parry's gang?"

Dunston nodded grudging approval. "You haven't
been entirely idle. Yes, Jeff Parry. Ringleader, chief of
the outlaw band. Arrogant bastard. I'd put a price on his
head, only he'd do the same to me, and his guns are
better than mine. A whole lot better.''

"That's why Mayfield?"

"Forget about Mayfield!" Dunston slapped his palm
against the desk.

Boyd sat down in one of the armchairs facing the
desk. Dunston, irked, said, "Make yourself comfort-
able.''

"Thanks, I will," Boyd said, stretching his legs.

Dunston picked a cigar from a desktop box, not of-
fering any to Boyd. He rolled it between thumb and
forefinger, making crinkling sounds.

Boyd said, "For a man who don't like trouble, you
sure picked a prize package in Dale Mayfield.''

Dunston said quickly, "You've seen him shoot?"

Boyd nodded. "He's fast, but moody. Watch out
when he gets in one of his moods.''

"Can he take Parry?"

"Yes, but not Concho."

The enthusiasm went out of Dunston. He settled back
in his chair, eyes gazing somewhere far away.

He said, "Concho! Always Concho. Nobody can beat
him to the draw.''

Eyes bright with malice, he asked Boyd, "Can you?"

"I'm no gunfighter.''

"What good are you then?"

Boyd said, "I'm the cattleman's friend. As long as he's a paid-up Association member, that is."

"What do you propose to do about the rustlers, friend?" The sarcasm was heavy on "friend."

"Put them out of business," Boyd said.

"Just like that, eh? How?"

"You don't want to know."

Dunston considered that, rolling the cigar under his nose, inhaling the aroma. Abruptly, he chuckled. "So that's how it is, eh?"

"What do you care, so long as the job gets done?"

"I don't. As far as I'm concerned, the only good rustler is a dead one."

"Well, then," Boyd said.

He folded his legs, feet flat on the floor. He leaned forward, forearms across the tops of his thighs.

He said, "Outlaws are only part of the problem. The other part is the crooked lawmen who let them get away with murder."

"LaRue," Dunston said. "He's in thick with Parry."

"That a fact?" Boyd inquired mildly.

"I just said so, didn't I?"

"Can you prove it?"

"I don't have to prove it, I just know it!"

"Oh," Boyd said. "There's a lot of funny things going on in town."

He mentioned some of them: the murder of Fred Bland, Wells Fargo agent and Cattleman's Protective Association representative; the failed stagecoach holdup, and the death of the guard, Randle; the blasting of the mine vault, and the disappearance of watchman Joe

Craigie. Other things, subtle items he'd noticed, Boyd
kept to himself.

He said, "Don't forget about the Hulls either, Oates
and especially Porter. And their black-sheep *compadre,*
Kingston. Tough bunch."

"They're sons of bitches, but they can be handled,"
Dunston said.

"They won't like it when Mayfield shows. Neither
will Parry. This could push things to a head."

"They're already at a head," Dunston said irritably.

"Besides," he added, "I'll have you to protect me."

"I'm a troubleshooter, Dunston, not a bodyguard."

"I know what you are."

"Whatever you think you know, keep it to yourself.
My job won't be any easier if word gets out that I'm
anything but Cattle Buyer Bowman."

"Think I'm a fool?" Dunston jeered. "Listen, Bowman—if that is your name—"

"It'll do," Boyd said.

"I could go to war with the rustlers. Hire an army of
guns and clean up on that Rock House bunch and their
friends in town. But I can't make any money that way,
apart from the fact that I might get killed myself. That's
a job for the Cattleman's Protective Association. If you
can't do it, what good are you?"

"The Association recognizes your right to be secure
in your person and property," Boyd said blandly.

Dunston stared. "What kind of bullshit is that? I want
results!"

"You'll get them."

Boyd rose. Dunston said, "Where are you going?"

"Back to work," Boyd said.

"What can one man do against Parry's gang and a bunch of badge-wearing crooks?"

"I'll surround them."

"Glad you can joke about it. Now."

Boyd said, "One more thing: I need to be able to come and go freely on your land."

Dunston looked at him. Boyd said, "If you want to catch rustlers, go to where they are. You've got the biggest herd."

"All right," Dunston said. "I'll fix it through my foreman, Bonner. That business about you being a cattle buyer should cover it, give you a reason for snooping around."

Boyd was thoughtful. Dunston said, "Bonner's my man. He knows how to keep his mouth shut."

"The less he knows, the less he has to keep shut."

Dunston scowled. "You like to push. Don't go thinking you've got me buffaloed. I let it pass because I'm humoring you." He made an airy wave with the cigar, a dismissive gesture.

"Odds are you'll be dead within the week," he added.

Boyd shrugged. "Nothing personal, Dunston. I'm just doing a job."

"Nothing personal here either. Hell, I hope you last out the week and then some. It'll save me the cost of shipping the body back to the Association's home office," Dunston said.

Movement outside the big window caught Boyd's eye. Two riders approached the ranch house at a gallop. Some ranch hands gathered to see what it was all about. The riders reined in hard, swinging down from their saddles before the horses were fully stopped.

Dunston stood, facing the window. "Now what?"

One of the riders made for the ranch house; the other stayed behind with the horses. The first man hurried across the open space ringed by outbuildings. He came almost at a run, head down, grim-faced. He came straight at the window, not showing any sign that he saw Dunston on the other side. A collision seemed imminent, but the path he was on took an abrupt right turn. He followed it, moving out of sight.

It was quiet in the room. The horses and men outside were too far from the window to be heard. A distant door slammed. Dunston sighed, letting the cigar die away.

Commotion in the hall, raised voices, clattering footfalls drawing nearer.

Outside the door, the footsteps stopped. A knock sounded, respectful yet firm.

Dunston shouted, "What?"

"Trouble, Mr. Dunston!"

Two men sat on the ground, back to back, hands tied behind their backs. They were dazed, bruised, and badly beaten.

"They ain't even rustlers," Bonner said contemptuously, "just plain ol' dumb cow thieves."

Rance Bonner, Dunston's foreman, was bearish, round-faced, with a gray-flecked Vandyke mustache-and-chin-whiskers combination.

A few miles west of the ranch house, in a hollow, an open field stood beside a stream. At this time of year, in late October, the stream was a thin trickling thread winding through a bed of round polished stones. It was

bordered by brown bramble bushes and dry golden
reeds. The stony field was matted with dusty strawlike
yellow-brown grass. Scattered bloodstains were so dark-
red that they were almost black. They led across the
ground to a wounded man who lay in the shade at the
field's edge, where a thicket grew. A cowboy, young,
barely out of his teens, lay on his back with his head
propped up against a fallen tree. A flannel shirt lay
folded under his head, as a pillow. He was pale, shivering. A blanket covered him from the shoulders down.
His boots stuck out of the bottom of the blanket. Two
buddies hovered over him, tending him. There wasn't
much they could do except reassure him that he was
going to be all right.

The cow thieves sat in the middle of the field, ringed
by Dunston and eight of his riders, all mounted. They
seemed a rough bunch for cowboys: Dunston's best
men. Boyd was there too, astride the gray. Seen from
horseback, looking down at them, the prisoners seemed
even meaner and more contemptible.

A wagon entered the scene, rumbling to a halt. The
wounded man—his name was Kyle—was loaded into it.
His face was white, waxy. Boyd thought he was dead,
or at least unconscious, but he cried out in pain from the
jostling when he was transferred to the wagon bed. One
of his friends hunkered down beside him.

The driver, whose stiff beard stuck out like a neck
ruff, still wore a white chef's apron.

Dunston said, "Take Kyle back to the ranch house
and send for the doctor, Cookie."

"He's been sent for, Boss. Doc Grinnell," the driver
said.

"Good," Dunston said. "Tell him Kyle was shot by a rustler and that's all."

"I know what to tell him, Boss."

"Good."

Cookie turned the wagon and started back toward the house. Dunston called after him, "Put Kyle in a guest room in the ranch house! Nothing's too good for a man who takes a bullet for Dunston!"

A thin cloud of dust humped along the trail in the wake of the departing wagon. The wagon vanished around a bend, the dust cloud lingering for a moment before fading away.

Dunston rode a big black mare. Its front hoofs pawed the dirt near the cow thieves.

"Now for you sons of bitches," he said.

The prisoners were downcast, shrunken.

"I know them," said Fyfe, a Dunston man. "Byers and DePugh. They work for Tanner over on Bobtail Creek."

Byers was beefy, blue-jowled, with thick brows meeting above his nose. DePugh, a youngster about Kyle's age, was fair-haired, wild-eyed, fine-boned.

Byers spoke thickly, through smashed lips. "Yeah . . . we ride for Tanner."

"Not no more," Fyfe said. "Tanner fired them for being lazy, thieving no-accounts."

Byers told Fyfe what he could do to himself. Bonner, on foot, backhanded Byers hard. Byers told Bonner the same thing. Bonner wound up for another blow.

"Hold your hand," Dunston said.

Bonner shrugged. Byers told Dunston what he could do to himself. Bonner gave a look that said, *See what happens when you slack off on these scum?*

Dunston said, "Which one of you shot my man?"

Byers told him to commit an unnatural act. DePugh said, "*He* did it! Byers!"

Byers laughed, a harsh croak. He said, "You dumb bastard, that won't help you now. Can't you see we're in for it?"

"You did it, Byers! You shot that man!"

"Sure, I did it, if it makes you any happier, kid."

Dunston said, "Who saw it? You, Jess?"

Jess, a cowboy with a ropy mustache, said, "*He* did it, Mr. Dunston. That punk kid." Meaning DePugh.

"You sure, Jess?"

"Yes, sir."

Dunston drew his gun and fired. The first shot hit the ground near DePugh's legs. He screamed. The second shot hit him below the knee. He fainted.

Byers, white-lipped, said, "What'd you do that for?"

"Justice," said Dunston.

"Sheeeeyit. Get on with the hanging, you white-haired son of a bitch."

"All right," Dunston said. "But not here."

Bonner said, "The tree?"

"Yes."

Some of the men started to get down from their horses. Bonner held up a hand. He said, "Whoa."

The men paused. Dunston said, "What's wrong?"

Bonner jerked a thumb at Boyd, saying, "What about him?"

"He's okay," Dunston said.

"I don't know him."

"I do."

Fyfe said, "Your say-so is good enough for me, Boss. How about the rest of you boys?"

Most of the others murmured agreement. Bonner said, "Always sucking up, ain't you, Fyfe?"

Fyfe started to say something. Bonner cut him off, saying, "Shut up."

Bonner was more amused than angered. He shrugged, saying to Dunston, "You're the boss."

"Damned right," Dunston said.

Bonner hooked one huge hand under Byers's arm and jerked him to his feet. Byers spat in Bonner's face, then grinned. Bonner struck him a tremendous blow in the face. Byers sagged. Bonner held him up with one hand.

Some of the men got down to help. Byers was lifted onto the saddle of his horse. He had to be held in place for a moment before he could sit without falling. De-Pugh, his leg shattered, was unable to sit his horse. He was tied face-down across it. The horse got the scent of blood and fear in its nostrils and was frightened.

"Not here," Dunston said.

They rode out, crossing the field at a diagonal to the northwest. Ahead were a series of ridges, long smooth slopes stretching away toward the mountains. A gap opened; through it the group rode, into a wide flat space dotted with cacti and brush. Dominating it was a large dead tree, stark, twisted, lightning-blasted. It was ten feet tall, its top jagged where the upper trunk had snapped off. Not far below, a pair of limbs jutted from its sides in the cruciform position. Its shape suggested a headless, handless corpse.

A hanging tree.

Boyd said, "Ain't got much use for the law, huh?"

"I'm the law," Dunston said.

Ropes, bright yellow hemp, were thrown over the tree limbs. The tree was silver-gray, like driftwood.

Dunston said, "If I turned them over to LaRue, he'd just turn them loose to steal again."

Boyd said, "What about Hull?"

"Those Hulls are all too cozy with the town businessmen for my liking. And Kingston is a notorious bandit and killer."

With mocking concern, Dunston added, "This bothers you, Bowman?"

"Hanging a man for stealing a cow is a hard thing, but a rancher's got to live too."

Byers's horse was led under a rope. John Morgan, hardbitten, thin-faced, fitted the noose around Byers's neck. Byers tried to spit in his face, but his mouth was too dry. He managed to spray Morgan with blood droplets from his pulped lips. Morgan snugged the noose, bringing Byers up short. The horse pranced nervously, Jess holding its reins.

On the other side of the tree chaos erupted. DePugh couldn't hang while lying tied face-down across his saddle. He was cut loose by Chino, a Mexican with Asiatic eyes and a thin wispy mustache. DePugh fell to the ground, screaming. The horse, already spooked, began trampling him. A handful of cowboys labored vainly to get the situation under control.

The horse upreared, eyes wild. The circle of men gave way and the horse broke free, bolting. It raced away. DePugh rolled around on the ground, shrieking.

Dunston frowned. "What's the problem over there?" He spoke loudly to be heard over the clamor.

"Sorry, Boss," Chino said.

Bonner stood nearby, hands folded across his chest, smirking. He started forward, rolling up his sleeves.

"You dumb asses," he said. "You've already wasted too much time."

He nudged DePugh with his boot toe, sending the wounded man into fresh writhings.

"You can't hang this idiot from a horse, not with that bum leg of his," Bonner said.

While Bonner was showing the others how DePugh should be hung, Boyd looked around, scanning the landscape. Something he always did. Habit. Survival habit.

The mountains were far. Nearer were some humpbacked ridges in the west. Motion crawled atop one of them. A blur of motion, and then it was gone. Like an insect. At that distance, a man on a horse would look like an insect. Boyd was the only one who had noticed. The others were involved in the hangings.

Had he seen something? Or was it the shadow of a cloud, skimming across the top of the ridge? He turned his head so it seemed he was looking elsewhere, away from the ridge. From the corner of his eyes he watched the ridge. He was good at that, watching something while appearing to be watching something else.

DePugh's agonies were suddenly choked off. Bonner had the noose around his neck.

Bonner said, "Tie the other end of this rope to a saddlehorn."

"Not my horse," Fyfe said.

"This hombre's spooking the horses," Chino said.

Bonner said, "Hoist him yourselves."

No movement on the rocky ridge top, no blurs. At the

place where the blur had been, there was a flash, a tell-tale glint, sharp and bright. Then it was gone.

Boyd estimated the sightlines from the ridge top to where he was. He rode to the other side of the tree so it was between him and the ridge top. The glint probably wasn't a sniper, but why take chances?

The hanging was about to begin. Dunston sat his horse facing the tree, ropes stretched across the limbs on either side. On the left, DePugh sprawled on the ground, a rope around his neck. The other end was gripped by Chino, Dobie, Fyfe, a fourth man, and Bonner. On the right, on his horse, Byers sat with his head in a noose, his back ramrod-straight. Jess held the reins. John Morgan sat on his horse beside Byers, holding the rope, steadying it.

Dunston cleared his throat. He spoke to the prisoners.

He said, "You tried to steal my cows and you shot my man, damn you!"

He nodded curtly.

John Morgan slapped the back of Byers's horse's rump, shouting. The horse leaped forward.

Bonner said, "Ho!"

He and the others hauled away at the rope like it was a tug-of-war at a picnic. When DePugh's kicking feet were above their heads, Bonner tied the rope to a tree.

DePugh and Byers died not from broken necks but from strangulation, a slow, nasty death.

Bonner stood with fists on hips, head thrust forward belligerently. "What you got to say about that, mister?"

"Not a thing," Boyd said.

"That's right, you don't say nothing to nobody."

Boyd lit a cigarillo. Dunston took the dead cigar from

his pocket, bit off one end, and spat it out. Boyd struck a match, leaning in the saddle to give Dunston a light. The flame was held rock steady, without a tremor. Dunston puffed, cigar tip glowing orange through the smoke.

He nodded thoughtfully. "Maybe you'll do after all."

"Thanks," Boyd said dryly.

"Bowman's okay, boys," Dunston said. "He's one of us."

Four

Sundown found Boyd in a high place. He lay prone in a notch on a hilltop overlooking the hanging tree. The hill was southwest of the flat. It was higher than the rocky ridge in the northwest where Boyd had earlier glimpsed the blur and the glint. Between the high hill and the ridge was a V-shaped gorge, fanning out, winding west and upward in long lazy S-curves. The slope was the gateway to the Whispering Hills, the foothills of the Los Viejos Mountains. The rustlers' royal road. A path through the hills led to a canyon where the rustlers penned their stolen herds. No pursuer had found that hideout and returned. Those who ventured too deep into the hills were killed or driven off by unseen snipers.

So much had Boyd known in advance, from studying reports and letters of complaint and petitions for help from Five Creeks ranchers to the Cattleman's Protective Association. Member ranchers, of course. Non-members were hard out of luck. Dunston wasn't the only one hol-

lering about what the rustlers were doing to him. His
neighbors were hollering too. Some anonymously, their
letters unsigned for fear of being killed.

Earlier, Dunston had told his men, "Bowman's got
free run of the ranch. Give him what he asks for, whatever it is." His words hardly registered on his men, still
caught up in the memory of the recent double hanging.
Bonner noticed, though. He was thoughtful, disliking
Boyd/Bowman while reconsidering his changed status in
light of Dunston's statement.

The group rode out, leaving the hanged men dangling
from the tree. They went east, out of the gap, into the
field by the stream. A ridge hid them from sight of any
observers on the humpbacked rocky ridge. Boyd said,
"Be on guard against reprisals. You hanged two rustlers
today, and the others might want to even up the score."

"They weren't Parry's men," Dunston said. "He
wouldn't even have bothered to spit on them. Their kind
has no friends to avenge them."

"Would you have hanged them if they were Parry's
men?"

"I'd have given it some thought," Dunston said. "I—
hey, where you going?"

Boyd peeled off from the others, turning the head of
his horse south. He said, "I want to look around. I'll be
in touch in a few days. Don't worry if you don't hear
from me for a while."

"I won't," Dunston said.

Boyd rode south, paralleling the ridge. Dunston and
company dwindled to a swarm of dots. Brown land,
white sky, yellow sun . . .

Boyd reached the south end of the ridge. There was

an open space a hundred yards wide and then the start of another low ridge. No other human was in sight. Boyd rode into the gap. On either side, low ridges stretched north-south, brown sluggish snakes. Broad, shallow troughs lay between the crests, each crest slightly higher than the one before. Open ground stretched east-west, a broad boulevard cutting the line of ridges at right angles.

Boyd entered the second long valley on the right, riding north. The gray picked its way through stony ground with a sure foot. At no time did the tops of the ridges reach more than twenty feet high. The horse plodded along.

Boyd looked back. The valley mouth was lost from sight. He stopped his horse, climbing down carefully. This was snake country. Did Gila monsters get this far north? He wasn't sure.

He tied the reins to a tree branch. He wore a side-gun. The other gun was in a saddlebag, the carbine in its holder. He took a pair of binoculars from a saddlebag, and hung the strap from his neck. He climbed the east ridge, advancing on his belly the last few yards to the top. He peered through the dried weeds at the crest. Land rolled away from him, grazing land, miles and miles of it. With naked eyes and through the binoculars, he scanned the scene, examining it minutely. No one was on his trail. The binoculars were Swiss-made, high-power optics. He was careful to keep them out of direct sunlight, for fear of telltale glints. He swept the horizon, noting key land forms, comparing them to their counterparts on the maps he had memorized. The maps were copies of charts made by the U.S. Army Corps of Topographical Engineers surveying expedition to the region in 1851; very detailed, and still unsurpassed. He had some of them on his person, but the only map he needed to refer to was the one in his head.

He got back on his horse and continued north, toward the place of the hanging. At no time since taking leave of Dunston had he been within the sightlines of the humpbacked ridge.

Twice more he stopped and scanned his surroundings before moving on. The ridges began to shrink as he neared the end of the long valley. At the end, they were little taller than the top of his hat. The ground dipped, becoming soft, wet. Hummocks shaped like half-domes rose on all sides, big as houses. The muddy patch wound through them, fed by a tiny spring.

The hanging tree was in a cup-shaped valley. Southwest of the valley were the mounds, nestled in the lee of the high hill at the mouth of the ravine.

Boyd studied the scene. The hanged men hadn't gone anywhere. They still dangled from the tree. He trained the binoculars on the humpbacked ridge, finding nothing out of the ordinary. Earlier he had seen a blur and a glint. Now, nothing. Daylight was waning.

He walked, leading his horse by the reins. The gray plodded along. They snaked through the mounds, emerging on the south side of the big hill. Between two rock buttresses a seam opened in the side of the hill. Boyd and the horse went up the slope to a ledge crowded with boulders and scrub brush. Boyd hid the gray in a thicket, tethering it to a stunted tree. There was cover and grass for grazing. Boyd equipped himself with the carbine, a box of shells, a canteen, the binoculars, and a thick chunk of dried beef.

He started up the hill. He didn't have to hang by his fingernails, but it wasn't an easy climb, especially not laden down as he was. He slung the carbine across his back to keep his hands free. The sun was low but still hot. He aimed for the notch in the top of the hill, reaching it after about ten minutes of hard effort. The notch was a hole where a piece had fallen out of the crest. It was a good covert. Well-shaded. The notch was a pool of shadows. Boyd lay prone in it, peering over the edge of the hill's north face.

The humpback ridge was on the opposite side of the ravine, and lower than the hill. Boyd looked down on it. A side-branch on the north side of the ravine curved like a hook, connecting with the humpbacked ridge. Boyd couldn't see too far into it. Its depths were hidden by rock overhangs.

He settled in to wait. Patience was the soul of the hunter. It was peaceful up there, away from people. *Not too far away,* he thought.

From time to time he glimpsed Dunston riders, stick figures flitting around distant herds. They were on the eastern flats, far from the ridges. The hanged men had been left as a warning to those who came from the hills by the rustlers' road.

A flash of movement nearby gave him a start. It came from the empty air, several hundred feet up. A buzzard, wheeling over the valley, over the hanged men. Others arrowed to the sight.

When he got thirsty, Boyd took a sip from his canteen. When he was hungry, he cut a strip of dried beef with his pocketknife and popped it into his mouth and chewed it. It took a lot of chewing.

Bugs chittered and clicked. The sun went down. Boyd was still chewing. That dried beef was tough.

Above the mountains the air quivered with a golden tawny blush. Afterglow. On the ground, royal purple shadows. It was so still that Boyd heard the fluttering wings of buzzards hovering over the site. They were getting bolder.

A head popped up from behind the top of the hump-backed ridge. Boyd reached for the binoculars. The head belonged to a man unknown to him. He looked tough. He scrambled around the ridge top, studying the valley from different angles. He had no binoculars. He did not look up at the high hill, Boyd's vantage point. Boyd could have tagged him with the carbine easy.

The man ducked back down out of sight, vanishing the way he came. Boyd resumed chewing.

A quarter hour passed. The sky was white, colorless. There was movement inside the hook-shaped side-branch. From it emerged two riders. One was the man on the ridge top. He was wolfish, wary, well-armed. His clothes were gray, brown, and tan. His companion was more of the same. Boyd didn't recognize him. Both men looked half-starved. Their horses were better fed than they were—only good common sense, for their lives depended on their mounts.

They rode side by side, slow, watchful, making for the hanging tree. A low-flying buzzard landed on top of it, establishing a prior claim. It croaked at the newcomers.

The riders neared the tree, horses skittish in the presence of death. The buzzard stood its ground, talons skittering against the dead wood of its perch. Its hairless head hunched down below its wings, eyes glaring.

Darkness grew. There were no stars. Overcast.

The ravine side-branch yielded a third rider. *Smart,* thought Boyd. *Held a man in reserve in case of trouble.*

Only one? Or was there a fourth man lurking in the side-branch?

The third man joined the others, whom he much resembled. They were rustlers, real ones, unlike the cut-rate variety now hanging from the tree. They'd come out of the hills earlier that day, just in time to witness the fracas between Byers and DePugh and Dunston's men. They'd taken cover in the side-branch, unseen and unsuspected, except by Boyd, who'd seen one or more of them spying on the hanging from the ridgetop. They'd remained hidden until now.

That was how Boyd figured it. There might be a few gaps, but it fit the facts as he knew them. That was why he'd doubled back to the hanging place and kept vigil.

Once Dunston's crew had left, the rustlers could have escaped in plenty of time with no danger. They hadn't. Why? To steal cattle? Bold thieves might strike now, when Dunston least expected it. Such boldness marked them as Boyd's meat.

The lookout, the second man, and the straggler. Three men. Three outlaws. Parry's men?

They talked for five minutes. Boyd couldn't make out the words. The others deferred to the second man. He gave the orders. He gave one to the straggler, the third man. The straggler obeyed reluctantly, getting off his horse and approaching the tree. The buzzard flapped its wings, beating them furiously. The straggler flinched. The others laughed. The straggler clapped a hand on his gun, only to unhand it at a short sharp command from the second man. Advancing on the tree, ignoring the angry beatings of the buzzard's big wings, the straggler drew his knife and cut down one of the hanged men.

The corpse thudded to the ground. The buzzard squawked and flew away.

In the east, a wagon rolled into view, emerging from behind a low ridge, coming from the direction of the distant ranch house. At first, Boyd heard it more than saw it. Sight and sound alike were muffled by thick woolen darkness. The wagon cut across the stream and angled across the field.

The valley was a bowl of blackness compared to the open ground. The rustlers could see wagon, outlined against a charcoal sky. Those on the wagon could not see the rustlers, or if they did, thought nothing of it, for they came on without a pause.

The rustlers took cover. The second man got off his horse and sheltered behind the hanging tree. The other two and the three horses disappeared among the rocks at the base of the humpbacked ridge.

The second man stood with his back to the tree, a gun in each hand. Boyd had a clear shot at him, not at the others. That didn't suit his plans. He could wait for all three to once more enter his line of fire, or he could move. Being the active type, he moved.

There was no way down the north face; he'd seen that upon first reaching the summit. He had to go down the way he came, along the south face. In the dark. Quietly.

He moved like flowing water, but it took time. The shooting was over well before he reached the bottom of the hill.

• • •

The wagon neared the tree, a freight wagon drawn by two horses in tandem, big, husky, hearty draught animals. The driver was Jess; beside him sat Fyfe. In the back of the wagon were digging tools, picks and shovels.

Fyfe said, "Bonner's got it in for me, sticking me on this stinking gravedigging job."

"You crossed him," Jess said. "What'd you think he was gonna do? Treat you like his long-lost brother?"

"Bah!"

"What I want to know is, why me? What am I doing here?"

"Someone's got to dig."

Jess yelped. "Wha—?! What'll *you* be doing?"

"Making sure you don't screw up," Fyfe said.

The horses snorted, balking. Fyfe said, "Can't you control them animals?"

"Smell of death. Gets to 'em," Jess said.

"I don't smell nothing!"

"You ain't no horse."

"No, and no horse's ass neither. Let's get this over and done with so we can get back to the bunkhouse," Fyfe said.

Jess suddenly looked startled. The horses stopped. Fyfe said, "Now what is it?"

Jess pointed, eyes staring. "Look!"

A lone corpse hung from the tree.

Jess said, "One of 'em's gone!"

Bucket Clark stepped out from behind the tree. He faced the wagon, a thick-bodied, black-bearded man with a gun in each hand.

Jess gasped. *"A ghost!"*

Fyfe cursed, reaching for his gun. Clark's bullet tore through him. Clark walked toward the wagon, shooting. He put two more slugs into Fyfe. Fyfe slumped, chest shattered, leaking. Clark shot Jess three times, emptying the revolver in his right hand. He switched to the gun in his left, hammering rounds into the inert bodies of the two cowboys.

He caught hold of the traces before the horses could bolt. He was gentling them when the others burst out from behind the rocks, dashing into the open with drawn guns.

"They're kilt without you two even firing a shot," Bucket Clark said.

He'd gained his name from the ability to drain a bucket of beer in one long pull. The others were Sim Odell and Steve Haycox. Odell had been the spy on the ridge top. His father had been one of the first to storm the fort at the military academy at Chapultepec when Winfield Scott had taken Mexico City. Steve Haycox was a left-handed draw.

Clark, Odell, and Haycox. Boyd heard them call each other by name as he sneaked up on them. His booted feet stepped as lightly as if he'd worn moccasins. The trio was preoccupied with what they were doing; they didn't hear him. They cut down the remaining hanged man, and hung up Fyfe and Jess.

Odell said, "That'll send that son-of-a-bitchin' Dunston a warning, by Christ!"

"And he won't be able to do a thing about it," Clark said smugly. "Not while we got hold of these two gallows birds! Turn 'em over to the law—the right law,

that is—and Dunston's looking at a murder charge! Two
of 'em!''

Haycox frowned, puzzled. "What for you want to do
that?''

"I don't," Clark said. "That's a last resort. As long
as Dunston does as he's told, the dead men stay secret,
see?''

"Dunston won't hold still for that kind of hiding."

"Then he'll stand trial for murdering these poor hombres.''

Haycox got stubborn. "No jury'll convict a rancher
for lynching a couple of cow thieves!''

"No, but a trial will tie his hands but good so he can't
make trouble.''

"I don't get it, Clark."

"You don't have to. Just do as you're told."

Haycox shook his head mournfully. "I don't like it.
Rustling's one thing, body snatching's another!''

"You don't have to like it either. Just do it," Clark
said.

Boyd walked into their lives, what few seconds were
left in them. He stepped out of the dark, leveling a six-
gun.

He said, "Turn around so I don't have to shoot you
in the back, boys. Looks better that way.''

They were turning, turning and drawing—drawing
against a drawn gun. None of them got off a shot. Boyd
fired three. The rustlers spun, flopped, fell dead.

Boyd reloaded, pocketing the spent brass. Not that he
had any doubt about being the only living human on the
scene. He was unsure before, but not now. Had there

been more than three rustlers, their *compadres* would have joined them for the ambush. Bucket Clark . . . Boyd knew that name. Clark was wanted in Texas, Oklahoma, and Kansas for killings and other crimes. Too bad Boyd couldn't collect the rewards on the outlaws, if any. That kind of notoriety he didn't need. It would interfere with his work.

Dunston must have had second thoughts about leaving the hanged men out in the open. He'd sent two men to bury the evidence—the digging tools in the wagon were proof of that. Now the two cowboys hung dangling from the tree while the hanged men were laid out in the wagon. Too bad. Boyd could have warned them by firing a warning shot into Clark, but then what? That left the other two rustlers alive and forewarned, with Boyd on the hilltop and his horse on the ground. No way he was giving up that much edge.

A hard night's work lay ahead. He cut down Fyfe and Jess, and removed the nooses around their necks. He took one by the heels and dragged him a half-dozen paces from the rustlers. The dead man stank. Boyd walked away from him, taking a few breaths of fresh air. He tied his bandanna over his nose and face. That helped some. He dragged the other dead cowboy, laying him out beside his partner. He tied halter ropes to the bridles of the team of horses hitched to the wagon. He freed them from the traces and hitched them to the tree.

Byers and DePugh had soiled themselves when hanged. Their flesh was cool and their limbs were stiffening. The nooses were buried deep in their necks. Black faces, swollen black tongues extended. Pop eyes—at least they hadn't been eaten by the birds. Boyd used his

knife to shorten the long trailing ropes, leaving only
three or four feet of hemp protruding from the top of
the noose. These men were hanged and bore the proof
of it. That might prove useful later.

In the back of the wagon were some old horse blan-
kets. Boyd wrapped up the hanged men in them.
Shrouds, probably brought for just that purpose. He tied
each one across the back of one of the horses from the
team. They didn't like it, but it had to be.

He found Jess and Fyfe's guns, both unfired. He fired
them into the air, emptying them. He put them in the
dead hands of their owners. A stranger happening on the
scene might well assume that the cowboys had stumbled
across the rustlers and shot it out. The wagon horses?
Stolen by survivors whose own mounts had fled during
the battle. Dunston and those of his men who had done
the hangings would know better, but they wouldn't shout
it to the world. They wouldn't know what had become
of the hanged men. Boyd's hand in the affair would
remain hidden, though Dunston might have his suspi-
cions.

It wouldn't do to be caught by Dunston's men or Parry's gang, either of whom could be nearby. Or both.
There had been shooting and sound traveled far. That
was why Boyd had waited to the last before firing the
dead men's guns. If others were nearby, the flurry of
shots would sound as the final fusillade of a gun battle.

Boyd stepped up into the saddle of the gray. Tied to
it were a pick and shovel from the wagon. They'd come
in handy later.

Was that the sound of distant hoofbeats? He'd spent
enough time here. He rode out, trailing a string of two

horses, each laden with a corpse. He left the way he
came, through the mounds in the southwest of the valley.
He kept the horses on a short rope, to avoid snags.
Among the mounds the way was dark, close. Rising
above them, blacker than the darkness, was the bulk of
the high hill. Boyd kept it on his right, using it to steer
by.

Wind rustled the tops of the bushes. A smell of rain
was in the air. Let it come, thought Boyd. It would help
hide his trail. In any case, trackers wouldn't be much of
a threat until daylight. Before then, he'd do what he
could to lose them. More dangerous was the chance of
stumbling into a party of night riders—rustlers or cowboys.

The mounds dropped below head height as he broke
into the long valley between the ridges. Hoofs scuffed
rock. The footing was better, allowing for steady progress. Boyd moved out, not too fast, putting some distance between himself and the hanging place. A few
turns of the valley put it out of sight.

He paused, listening. The hoofbeats he thought he had
heard before were gone. Perhaps the riders had gone
away, perhaps they had never existed at all. But Boyd
wasn't the type to hear things that weren't there. Whatever he'd heard was now silent.

He rode on. Breezes lifted his hat brim. They were
cool, moist, a rarity in this arid land. Saguaro cacti,
many taller than a man, dotted the valley floor. In the
upper limbs of one sat an owl, motionless but for the
turning of its head as it watched Boyd pass by. A little
farther on, a field mouse darted into the open, crossing
Boyd's path. There was a beating of wings as the owl

swooped down on its prey. With its wings extended, it was damned big. It skimmed the ground, flying away with the mouse wriggling in its talons.

From behind came a distant clamor. Boyd looked back. A weak glow flashed from behind the hills enclosing the hanging place. Dunston's men?

Boyd neared the south end of the long valley. Amid the murk there was sound, motion. That wasn't so good. Dunston's men were liable to shoot, not talk. Boyd wasn't in the mood for either. If they were Dunston's men . . .

Boyd halted on the east side of the valley, where a handful of waist-high rocks provided some kind of cover. He made sure that the horses were securely hitched to some thick roots jutting out of the side of the ridge. He unsheathed the carbine and climbed the ridge, keeping low, not skylining. Near the top he got down on hands and knees, low-crawling, flattening dry weeds beneath him.

He crawled south for some yards, hidden by the weeds. Parting them, he peered beyond the end of the valley, where it was met at right angles by a dry wash. Scattered in the open was the source of disturbance, hulking shapes with hoofs and horns: cattle. Only a few, for the wash was far from water and good grazing land.

From his vantage point Boyd reconnoitered the area. It seemed safe. He went back to the horses. Lights flashed in the air above the hanging place, like summer lightning. They were no closer. Whoever was there was in no hurry to go charging off into the darkness in search of survivors of the shootout.

Boyd rode out of the valley. The cattle moved aside,

not scared, just cautious. The three-horse train angled southeast across the wash, entering a valley west of the front ridge. According to the maps, the valley was open at its southern end. The maps were almost forty years old, but there was no reason for the valley to have been closed since. If it was, the ridge was not so steep that Boyd couldn't cross it, except for his dislike of outlining himself as he topped the crest.

He pushed through the valley at a faster clip than before, less worried about being heard so far from the hanging place. The south end was indeed open; it gave on a broad empty slope, empty of all other horses and men. Barring any bad luck, he was in the clear.

As he started forward, the first drops of rain began to fall.

Five

Boyd buried the bodies before dawn. The burying place was a sugarloaf butte southwest of Dunston's spread, on unclaimed land bordering a neighbor's tract. Unclaimed because neither rancher wanted it. Stony, sandy ground, with little grass and no water. It was off the beaten paths of even the rustlers.

At the foot of the butte's south face was a cleft in the rock: the grave. It was delta-shaped, point-up, about five feet high, four feet wide, and three feet deep. The site was in a hollow, hidden from view. There was light, but not enough to cast a shadow. Thick grayish-white mist hung over all, adding to the dreamlike unreality.

Inside their blanket shrouds, the bodies were stiff. Boyd shoehorned them into the hole. Their limbs were stiff, unresponsive. He used the spade to break them so they'd fit better. The bodies were jammed together, knees up. It was warm work. Boyd's jacket was off, his shirt sleeves rolled up. Mist, warm as sweat, beaded on his flesh. He wore gloves, no hat. The hat rested on a nearby rock.

He filled the cavity with stones, big ones, each as big as a paving stone or bigger. It took plenty of them, but they would discourage varmints from digging up the dead and eating them.

He covered the stones with dirt. Topsoil, so the covering would be the same color as its surroundings. He uprooted some small bushes, sticking them in the grave dirt so they'd look as if they'd grown there.

The job done, he took a break. He stretched, working the kinks out. Hard work was no bother. He was used to it. He'd been a rancher.

He breakfasted on dried beef and canteen water. A smoke would have been good, but he held off. He rolled down his sleeves, and put on his jacket and hat. The hat didn't feel right. He punched out the crown from the inside and bent the brim. It still didn't feel right, but he kept it on.

He rode out, still trailing two horses. They were easier now, relieved of their burden of dead men. The route crossed long flat stretches of rock, blanking out his trail. The signs were there for those who know how to look, but few if any were likely to come this way. Boyd had spent the better part of the night erasing his trail to throw off all pursuers.

Now, he went south, then southeast. Haze covered the scene like a grounded cloud. It splintered, sectioning into swirling banks. Objects took shape, outlining into ridges, rocks, trees. Staking out a far-flung landscape. Gradually becoming three-dimensional.

The sun rose, burning off the haze. Breezes lifted, warm, too brief. Gray sky.

When he was far enough away from the butte, he got rid of the tools, the pick and shovel, dumping them in a weedy ditch.

Riding on, he lit up a smoke. It tasted good.

Later, he cut the two spare horses loose. They ran away. They'd find their way home.

Slickrock River ran diagonally across the basin, from northwest to southeast. Dunston occupied the choice acreage on the upper half, centered around the Crossing. Five creeks came out of the west to join the river. The fourth creek to the south bordered Brent's ranch. It marked the northern edge of his property. The land nestled at the foot of the western hills. The cliffs were unbroken here, no mountain passes. A buttress thrust out from the cliffs at right angles for a mile or more, forming the southern boundary.

Brent was stocky, with a thick black mustache shaped like an upside-down canoe. He and Boyd sat on the ranch house verandah, drinking. A wooden awning protected them from the midday sun. The chairs were straight-backed, armless. Brent sat facing the back, arms resting across the top of the chair, glass in hand. Boyd sat with his feet up on the rail, tilting the chair back on two legs.

Brent said, "You're up against a marked deck, Mr. Bowman."

Boyd nodded, encouraging the other to go on, while not necessarily agreeing with him.

Brent said, "The cattle business hereabouts is sewed up."

"By who?"

"The Flagstaff crowd. Big buyers."

"Not so big that they can't make room for one more, Mr. Brent."

"No?" Brent was too polite to smile, so he just nodded.

"My money's as good as anyone else's," Boyd said.

"It's not a matter of money."

"What then?"

"Power," Brent said. "You're bucking a combination."

"What, a bunch of dude cattle buyers? I can handle them."

"They play rough," Brent warned.

"What are they doing to do, shoot me?"

"I wouldn't care to go up against them," Brent said.

"Forget about them for a minute," Boyd said. "Let's talk about you. You want more money for your cattle. I'll pay more. I smell a deal in there somewhere, Mr. Brent."

"Call me Brent. Everybody does, even my wife."

"Frank, Brent," Boyd said.

Brent nodded, rising. "You're not from around these parts, Frank."

"No, West Texas," Boyd said.

Brent nodded, as if that explained things. Texans were mavericks, none more ornery than those from west of the Pecos. Their reputation was far-flung.

Earlier, Boyd had ridden into the ranch. It was small, modest in comparison to Dunston's. Brent was a rancher, not an empire builder. Boyd rode in slow and easy. Brent's hands, what few there were, saw Boyd coming from a long way off. Before he neared, they rode in to the ranch. They were waiting for him when he arrived. They were dismounted, grouped near the corral, some leaning on the fence. Elaborately minding their own business, not hostile, not friendly. Watchful. As was Brent. Boyd introduced himself as Frank Bowman, would-be cattle buyer. He knew cattle. So did Brent. That gave them something to talk about. At lunchtime, they were still talking, so Brent invited him to join the feed. Brent's wife was plain-faced, but she could cook. There was a brood of kids, reasonably clean, all wearing shoes.

Afterwards, Brent and Boyd sat outside, with a bottle between them and glasses full. Boyd sipped whiskey from the tumbler, each sip a rattlesnake's kiss. He liked the bite. Not too many sips set his head buzzing. Brent barely touched lips to his.

Now, Brent said, "Mind if I ask a personal question, Frank?"

"Go ahead."

"Got a family?"

Boyd shook his head. "A brother, and some distant kin, that's all."

"A family ties your hands, Frank. That's not an excuse, it's a fact. Or maybe it is an excuse, but if it is, it's a good one."

"The best," Boyd said.

"All I know is, I sell my stock in Flagstaff, and so do does everybody else, even Dunston. At buyer's rates. Enough to scrape by for another year, so I can start it up all over again," Brent said.

"That bad, huh?"

Brent nodded. "There's money in it. Big money, for the buyers and their friends."

"Sounds kind of exclusive."

"It is. And worth killing for. Killing you, not me," Brent said. "They don't need to kill me. I do what I'm told. I've got a family."

Boyd said, "What if all the ranchers stood together?"

"It'd mean a showdown. It hasn't come to that. Probably never will."

Boyd shrugged. Brent gestured toward the ranch house, forgetting the tumbler of whiskey in his hand. Some slopped out of the top, spilling. Brent blinked, surprised.

He said, "Damn! That's a waste of good whiskey."

He tossed back the rest, getting red in the face, watery-eyed. "At least that won't go to waste," he said, shuddering.

He said, "See these walls? Stone! There's plenty of timber on the slopes, enough to build hen houses, but I built with stone. Why? Because stone doesn't burn. Handy when the Apaches were on the warpath. They're gone now, finished. It's better now, but still bad."

He shook his head, disgusted. "Why tell you my troubles? Pardon the bellyaching, Frank."

"I wouldn't call it that," Boyd said.

"No? What would you call it?"

"Good sense."

"Yeah, well, you can get damned good and tired of it," Brent said.

He uncorked the bottle and filled his glass with whiskey. Boyd didn't say anything. Hell, it was the man's whiskey. He had a right to drink it.

He exercised that right.

He said, "Don't mind me, Frank. Sometimes I get sore."

"Like now?"

"Maybe. What's it to you?"

"Not a thing," Boyd said mildly. "Appreciate the hospitality, Brent. I'll leave before I wear out my welcome."

"Have a drink."

"Thanks, I'm fine."

"I'll have one then."

And he did.

A pale presence fluttered into the edges of the scene, nervous, angular: Mrs. Brent. She wore a moth-brown dress. She fretted, wringing her hands.

Brent saw her, frowned, then made like he hadn't seen her. He gulped whiskey. She sighed loudly. Brent's face couldn't have been any redder, but his neck began to swell.

"A fine host I am, driving you off with my talk! Don't mind me," he said.

Boyd said, "What about the Cattleman's Protective Association?"

Brent frowned, irked, puzzled. "What about it?"

"Maybe you should join up. They'd help you."

"Hah! Hell, Frank, I've been a member for years!"

Boyd knew that, but he was playing dumb, stringing him along.

Brent said, "Most Five Creeks ranchers belong to the Association, for what it's worth. Fred Bland couldn't protect himself, never mind about no cattle, Lord rest his soul."

"Bland? Who's he?"

"The Association man in Smoke Tree. He was," Brent said.

"Came to a bad end, did he?"

"Shot in the back," Brent said, sad. He held a glass in one hand and the bottle in the other. The glass was empty. He drank from the bottle but held on to the glass.

Boyd said, "Who killed him?"

"Who?"

"The man you were telling me about, Brent, the dead man."

"Oh, him!"

"Who killed him?"

"Who knows?" Brent looked canny. "I've got some ideas, though. A lot of funny business in town, and outside, too. The things I could tell you—"

"Brent!"

The shout came from Brent's wife, shrill with latent hysteria. The cords stood out on her neck, tense, vibrating.

That got Brent's attention, sobering him some.

His wife quivered like a plucked guitar string.

Boyd said, *"Saludos."*

He drank whiskey, draining the glass. He set it down on top of the porch rail. He went down three stone steps. Out from under the awning shade it was hot—hotter. The whiskey hit in mid-brain, hammering, straining the seams of his skull. He shivered.

He said, "That sure was a fine feed, Miz Brent."

She nodded, a quick birdlike bob.

"Nice talking to you, Brent. See you," he said.

He crossed the yard, angling toward the stables. Brent watched him go. Mrs. Brent watched Brent. Neither of them moved.

Boyd reappeared, on his horse. He nodded to the Brents, touched two fingers to his hat brim in a salute, turned, and rode away.

Horse and rider shrank, dwindling to a blur.

"I talk too damned much," Brent said.

"Drink too much, you mean!" his wife said.

He threw away the bottle, tossing it as far as he could. It hit the barn, not breaking.

Brent said, "You happy now?"

"No," Mrs. Brent said.

A map is not the territory. Boyd liked to see things for himself, get the feel of a place. Know the hunting grounds. Terrain mastery could mean the difference between life and death.

Leaving Brent's ranch, Boyd angled south. The long rock buttress marked the midpoint of the basin's southwest corridor. Boyd drifted into the lower half. Long low slopes were covered with short, dry, yellow grass. Where the grass was worn away, brown dirt showed.

Boyd crossed the last, southernmost creek. It was thin, a trickle.

An upright trident shape spiked the horizon. A three-horned peak, one of Los Viejos, the Old Ones, it shouldered aside the hills to wedge itself on the flat. Somewhere on its lower slopes lay Rock House, the rustlers' stronghold.

Boyd trained the binoculars on it. Overcast screened

out any telltale sunbeam from reflecting off the optics. The mountain was too far away to make out any details.

He rode on, keeping the low curving hills between him and the mountain. Often he paused, scanning the scene to familiarize himself with the landscape. The mountain demanded a closer look, but not now.

He trailed east, following a lazy winding course. In late afternoon, he came to Callan's ranch.

The ranch house was little more than a long shed. The roof sagged in the middle, almost touching the porch. The outbuildings were rickety shacks. All the structures were unpainted wood, sun-bleached and wind-scoured to a rich silver-gray color. The outhouse was too near the house. Livestock were few, gaunt, and weary.

Callan was marginal. No Association member either, Boyd recalled.

Callan was a middle-aged man with a young wife. A passel of kids whooped it up in the yard, noisy, dirty, and barefoot. Only the youngest resembled the wife, dark and moon-faced. The missus was in a family way, her belly swollen.

Boyd fed Callan the Frank Bowman line, that he was an independent cattle buyer looking to break into the local market. Callan didn't scoff. He thought it was a great idea, just what the stockmen needed. He, Callan, would welcome such a deal. He'd personally guarantee to deliver so many head of stock at such-and-such a price come next year's round-up. A few dollars in advance now would seal the bargain.

"I don't know," Boyd said, shaking his head. "I'm starting to sour on prospects in the basin."

"It's good cattle country," Callan said quickly.

Boyd looked around. The plains were dotted with a sparse scattering of cattle. He said, "What about rustlers?"

Callan, taken aback, said, "What about them?"

"I hear they're a real problem."

Callan was uneasy, evasive. "I don't know nothing about that."

"You don't? Ain't you never plagued by cow thieves?" Boyd was openly skeptical, disbelieving.

"Sure, I lose a few head every now and then," Callan said. "Everybody does."

"That bothers me."

Callan shrugged. "That's the price you got to pay."

"The law doesn't seem too eager to crack down," Boyd said.

Now it was Callan's turn to scoff. "Crack down on their pals? Not hardly!"

"But you don't have to worry about that," he added, brightening. "You're the buyer, not the stockman!"

"What if they steal the cattle after I buy them?"

"That won't happen."

"Uh-huh," Boyd said.

He and Callan stood behind the back of the barn, where the yard stretched to the horizon. In the middle ground, a road ran east-west. Beyond rose a whale-shaped mound, the ruins of a long-forgotten fort.

Out of the southeast a speck came crawling, inching past the mound toward the road. The speck became a blur, the blur became a horse and rider.

The rider crossed the road and made a beeline for the ranch. After some moments, his progress was virtually nil. He and the horse might well have been painted figures. They moved at a snail's pace.

The rider neared, a scarecrow slouched on a starving horse.

"That boy's done some hard riding," Boyd said.

Callan was silent, fidgeting, nervously plucking at a fold of his trousers.

The horse stumbled forward, its head down, near the ground. It had been ridden near to death. The rider was gangly, long-limbed. Grimy, filthy, clothes in tatters. Clutching the top of the saddlehorn was a pair of long-fingered, skeletal hands. In them were the reins.

Boyd said, "Know him?"

"I—ain't sure," Callan said.

He might have been telling the truth. Dirt streaked the rider's face, masking his features. Slitted eyes were alive with brightness.

Horse and rider looked straight ahead, oblivious to their surroundings. The horse plodded into the yard, making for a water trough. It lurched, staggered, fell forward on its knees.

The rider pitched forward, tumbling out of the saddle, sprawling on the hard ground, where he lay motionless.

The horse tried to rise, couldn't. It made distressed noises.

The rider stirred, got his legs under him, and crawled away from the horse, to the trough. His hat was still on, the fall having jammed it tight to his head. A black parson's hat, its round flat brim curling at the edges.

A gun was holstered on his hip. It was less dirty than the rest of him.

He clung to the side of the trough, resting. A final effort, and he chinned the trough, face poised over slimy green water. He plunged in head-first, up to the neck.

He splashed around happily. The horse moaned. It was making the other horses nervous. Boyd crossed to the gray, hitched to a corral fence top-rail. The animal made small mincing steps, fidgeting. Boyd put it between him and the stranger. He spoke softly to it, gentling it with his hands. He steadied a saddlebag, reaching inside.

The stranger surfaced, minus a hat. Long green strands of slime clung to his head and shoulders. Water ran off him. His shoulders heaved. Was he crying? No, laughing. He flopped to the ground, rolled on his back. He sat up, back against a fence post, legs spread in the dirt. He wasn't laughing.

Water had washed some of the dirt from his face. He was young, just out of his teens. Horse-faced, bucktoothed, sneering. Callan recognized him.

"Chris Yard!" he said, not overjoyed.

Yard nodded. He rose, using the post as a brace. He was a bit shaky on his feet. He clung to the post for support. He turned his face to the way from which he had come. A thin brown feather of dust showed against the sky. He studied it, frowning, rubbing his chin.

Callan nodded to his wife. She shooed the children into the ranch house, followed them inside, and slammed the door behind her. Yard nodded as if that suited him too.

He turned toward Boyd, still standing beside the horse. "That's a fine-looking animal, mister. Want to sell?"

"No," Boyd said.

"I won't take no for an answer," Chris Yard said. He was smiling, but so what?

Callan said quickly, "You can have one of mine, Chris."

"You got nothing worth taking," Chris Yard said. He looked back, over his shoulder. The dust cloud loomed a little closer.

Boyd said, "You sound like a man in a hurry."

"That I am," Chris Yard said. "You won't sell?"

"No."

Chris Yard shrugged. "That's okay, I got no money anyhow. So, I'll just take it."

He reached for his gun, not even a fast draw, as if he had all the time in the world. Boyd didn't have to draw. A gun was already in his hand, the gun he had taken from his saddlebag and been holding just out of sight behind the horse. He leveled it on Yard and fired.

The bullet shattered Chris Yard's right shoulder, spinning him. The gun leaped from his dead hand. When he realized he wasn't dead, he started screaming.

Boyd came out into the open, covering Chris Yard. He needn't have bothered. Chris Yard was tamed.

Callan, gaping, said, "What'd you do that for?!"

"I don't like walking," Boyd said.

Chris Yard kicked and thrashed, tearing up the dirt like a chicken with one wing down. Boyd picked up Yard's gun and unloaded it, scattering the shells. He tossed it away.

He eyed Yard's wound. Serious, not fatal. Bones were smashed, the arm dead from the shoulder down. Yard carried on, whooping and hollering. Irritated by the noise, Boyd positioned himself to lay the pistol barrel across Yard's skull and cool him out. Yard saw the weapon lining up on him and assumed the worst. He froze, paralyzed, struck dumb.

Boyd placed a finger across his lips. "Shhh . . ."

Yard shrank into himself, nodding, eyes bulging. Boyd said pleasantly, "You'll live."

"For now," he added.

Yard would keep for a while. Boyd went to the trough. In it was Yard's hat, submerged. Boyd took it, holding it upside down so the crown was full with water. He set it down before the fallen horse, under its nose. The horse drank.

Callan said, "Why'd you do it?"

"Poor animal was thirsty," Boyd said.

"No, why'd you shoot Yard? Now, we're in for it!"

He pointed at the dust cloud, now looming large. Beneath it was a wedge of mounted men, coming fast.

Six

Armed with a carbine and two guns, Boyd awaited the riders.

Callan said, "I don't want no trouble!"

"That's a good one," Boyd said.

The riders neared, a half dozen of them. Boyd recognized them as part of the posse that had set out from Smoke Tree two nights before. He lowered the carbine, holding it under his arm with the muzzle pointing down. Not too far down.

The posse reined in. They had done some hard riding. Their faces were cold, unfriendly. Their leader was Olcott, LaRue's deputy. He took in the scene, saying, "What's this?"

He got down from his horse and scowled at Boyd. Callan, anxious, said, "It's none of my doing!"

The wounded man crawled away, using his good arm and legs to drag himself painfully across the ground. Olcott crossed to where he could see the crawler's face.

He told the others, "It's Chris Yard."

That set off some muttering and hard-eyed looks from the posse.

In the interim, Yard's horse had risen to all fours. It stood with its snout in the trough. Olcott raised its left rear hoof, examining it.

He found what he was looking for. His dull-eyed gaze brightened.

"Missing part of a shoe, like the one we've been tracking," he said. "Yard's our man, boys."

The posse relaxed, breaking out grins. Olcott loomed over Yard. Yard cowered, whimpering. Olcott grabbed him by the back of the neck with one hand and hauled him to his feet, not gently. Yard was near fainting with the pain. Olcott held him at arm's length, Yard's feet off the ground. The massive Olcott showed no sign of strain.

He said, "You sonofabitch."

His free hand became a fist, smashing Yard in the face, splashing his features. Knocking him out.

Yard went limp. Olcott dragged him to the watering trough and dumped him in. Held his head underwater. Bubbles streamed to the surface. Yard kicked. Olcott held him under until the kicking stopped, grabbed a handful of hair, and hauled him out. Yard lay in a wet heap at his feet. Olcott wiped his hand on his pants.

"Butch Randle was my friend," he said.

He eyed Boyd, Callan. "What happened?"

"He tried to steal my horse," Boyd said.

"You shot him?"

"Yes."

"You done good. He's wanted for robbery and murder," Olcott said.

He studied Boyd. "I know you," he said, frowning. "You're . . ."

Olcott groped, drawing a blank on the name. Boyd supplied it for him.

"Bowman," he said.

"Bowman, right. You were on the stagecoach, the one Yard tried to rob," Olcott said. "Funny, you turning up here to meet him."

"He's not laughing," Boyd said, indicating Yard.

"Me neither. What are you doing here, Bowman?"

"Making the rounds. I'm a cattle buyer. I've been visiting the Five Creeks ranches for the last two days."

"Cattle buying, with the herds thinned and winter coming on?"

"Scouting for next year's prospects. If they look good, I'll be back with cash money when it's buying time."

"Could be," Olcott said.

His brow furrowed, his gaze turned inward. He was thinking. Finally, he said, "You did right to shoot this rascal."

"My pleasure," Boyd said.

The crisis was past. The others of the posse got down from their horses and gathered around Chris Yard, grinning and joking. They were all of the same type: cowboys, hunters, a rough and ready crew.

Olcott said, "We've been on the trail for two days.

How about some grub for me and the boys, Callan?''

"I'll see what I can do," Callan said.

A posse man said, "T'hell with the grub, bring us whiskey!"

Callan went to the ranch house, where his wife stood in the doorway, a toddler clinging to her skirts. A hurried talk, then he followed her inside.

Boyd took out a cigarillo, lit up. Olcott came alongside, saying, "Thanks for not killing him."

"I would have, but I missed," Boyd lied.

"We cut his trail yesterday morning, at North Pass. Been following him since. Sometimes we'd see him, too far away to make out his face. His horse lost part of a shoe, leaving a one-of-a-kind sign. It slowed him, but he had a pretty good start on us. If he'd have got a fresh horse, he'd have slipped us sure."

"Who is he?"

"Chris Yard. One of the maggots from the manure pile up at Rock House. That's where you'll find most of the local cow thieves," Olcott said.

He shook his head. "Rustling wasn't enough for Yard and his pals. They had to try robbery and murder. He'll hang for it."

Boyd exhaled smoke. "What about the others?"

"One's dead, two got away," Olcott said. "Maybe Yard feels like talking."

He bore down on Yard, who lay coughing and choking. He put his boot toe under Yard, flipping him over on his back. He put a foot on Yard's chest.

A couple of kids, the older ones, came outside to see what was happening.

Yard was played out. Green slime and bloody froth

clung to the corners of his mouth. His shoulder wound was raw, ugly.

Olcott put some weight on Yard's chest. Yard writhed, gurgling. Olcott said, "Who was with you in the holdup?"

"Not me," Yard gritted. "You got the wrong man—"

Olcott moved his foot near Yard's wound and put on the pressure. Yard screamed. Olcott eased up.

He said, "Don't lie, boy, or you're going to be in a world of hurt."

Yard wouldn't talk. Olcott ground his boot heel into Yard's flesh. Yard shrieked, then went inert. He didn't move, no matter what Olcott did to him.

"Playing possum," a posse man said.

Olcott shook his head. "Fainted."

"Give him another dunking."

In the wings, Callan was waiting. Now that the torture had reached a lull, he announced that food was served. His wife was setting down pots and platters on an outdoors trestle table, not far from the ranch house kitchen.

Olcott said, "You go, I ain't hungry."

His men whooped, and fell on the food. Olcott and Boyd were alone with Yard, who was still out.

Olcott said, "You might be in line for a reward. Wells Fargo."

"That might be dangerous, claiming it with some of the gang still on the loose," Boyd said.

"Think they'll lift a finger to help their pal? Think again. They'll leave him to hang while they run as far and fast as they can."

"No honor among thieves?"

"Hell, no. Especially not these varmints," Olcott said.

Boyd looked at him. "You know them?"

"I got an almighty powerful suspicion," Olcott said. "Yard, here, I got nailed dead to rights. Wick Osmond's just plain dead. That makes Clete Skraggs the third man, since him, Yard, and Osmond always ride together. What's got me stumped is the fourth man. But Yard knows, and I got him."

Boyd said, "Those are two tough hombres!"

"How so?"

"They botch the stagecoach holdup, double back to town, and blast the mining company vault while the posse's tearing up the territory looking for them."

Olcott was smug, superior. "That's what you think, huh?"

"That's what I heard," Boyd said.

"Let me tell you something. I cut the robbers' trail at first light, before anybody else. And I read sign real good. There were three sets of tracks. Two went south: Yard and somebody else, probably Skraggs. Yard's horse lost part of a shoe and couldn't keep up. The other got away, for now."

"And the third set of tracks? Where did they go?"

"That's a funny one. They went back to town."

"Hmm," Boyd said. "What do you make out of that?"

"Not a damned thing. Yet."

"The mine vault was blown to pieces."

"I know. We ran into a search party yesterday, told us what happened. Sheriff split us up, took half the men back to town to join the hunt. The rest of us kept dogging the robbers," Olcott said.

Boyd's cigarillo was burned down to a stub. He flipped it away. It arced to the ground, splashing orange sparks where it struck. He took out another cigarillo, paused, then offered it to Olcott.

He said, "Smoke?"

"I don't like them skinny little cigars," Olcott said.

Boyd shrugged, rolling the cigarillo in his fingers, hearing the faint rustling crackle of the leaf.

Boyd said, "Four robbers, and only one made it back to town."

"That's right."

"That mining deal was a big job for one man, unless he had help. That missing guard, maybe. Craigie, his name was."

Olcott snorted. "Joe Craigie? He's too dumb to steal."

"Too bad for him. In that case, he's probably dead."

"What do you care?"

Boyd bit off the end of the cigarillo, spat it out. "What if that gold wasn't blown up?" he said.

From behind their film of dullness, Olcott's eyes grew hot and bright. His hand shot out, battening on Boyd's left forearm. He said, "What are you trying to say?"

"Let go of my arm and I'll tell you," Boyd said.

Olcott obeyed, not out of fear but from greed. Boyd's arm was numb where Olcott had gripped it.

He clenched and unclenched his fist, flexing the muscles to restore circulation.

"The gold," Olcott said.

"All that gold, blown to atoms by a clumsy dynamiter," Boyd said. "You believe that?"

Olcott, breathing hard, fought the urge to lay hands on Boyd. "I don't get it, Bowman. What's your game?"

Meal over, the others started drifting away from the table, slowly filtering back toward the horses. Nearer, Yard showed signs of life, twitching and moaning.

Boyd said, "If there's a reward on him, you take it."

Olcott, instantly suspicious, said, "Why?"

"I don't want it."

"I know what you want," Olcott said. "Gold!"

Boyd set fire to the cigarillo and vented smoke. "What gold?" he asked innocently.

Before Olcott could reply, some of the posse men came within earshot. He broke off, saying, "I'll talk to you later, Bowman."

"I'll be around."

"Damned right you will."

A posse man said, "You didn't miss much, Olcott. I'm still hungry."

"A mighty poor feed," said another.

Their bellies full, or as full as they were going to get at Callan's, most of the posse men were eager to be away. Olcott was for pushing after the other fugitive, or said he was.

"Hell, he's long gone to Rock House," somebody said.

All eyes turned to Three-Horn Mountain, beneath which lay Rock House, too distant to be seen. The sun was low, shadows were long.

A man said, "Be dark soon. We don't want to go poking around there at night."

That met with general approval. It didn't take much to persuade Olcott to change course.

"We'll head back," he said.

Now the manhunters were eager to quit the scene. Olcott said, "Patch up Yard so he don't bleed to death on us."

Yard's wound was serious, but no life-threatening veins or arteries had been hit. A spare shirt from somebody's blanket roll was cut into strips for bandages. Yard's wound was bound up, he was hoisted into a saddle and tied in place so he wouldn't fall off.

Boyd mounted up. Olcott said, "Where do you think you're going?"

"Smoke Tree," Boyd said.

"All right then."

The posse was ready to go. Olcott said, "Better take your family to town, Callan."

"It's all right," Callan said.

"Yard's friends might come looking for him."

"I didn't do nothing."

Olcott shrugged, urging his horse forward. Callan followed on foot, saying, "They won't bother me. I know them Rock House boys. They're rowdy, sure, maybe a little wild—a lot wild, some of them—but deep down inside, where it counts, they ain't really bad.

"Besides, I ain't worth killing," he added.

He sounded unsure, as if trying to convince himself.

At nine o'clock at night the posse neared Smoke Tree. The road ran east-west, becoming Mercado Street in the town proper. A rise hid Smoke Tree, but its lights glowed in the sky above. Silhouetted against it was a church steeple.

Olcott steered the posse off the road, turning south. They circled the back of the graveyard, curving east into town. They slipped into the outskirts unobserved. Ahead lay Grand Street, running north-south. On the other side of it was Mextown, a cluster of adobe cubes, hazy with the smoke of cooking fires.

The posse turned north, parallel to Grand. The first cross street was Burnett. Squatting on the south side of Burnett was a flat-roofed stone blockhouse with barred windows, the jail.

Olcott halted the group behind the back of the jail. He did not dismount, but sent a runner inside. The runner returned with Assistant Deputy Joslyn.

Olcott said, "Is Wade back yet?"

"He is, but he ain't here," Joslyn said.

"Where is he?"

"Taking care of some personal business, if you know what I mean," Joslyn said, leering.

"That redhead over to the hotel?"

"Yeah." Joslyn licked his lips. "Nice, huh?"

Olcott ignored the comment. "He catch anybody?"

"Just her. Looks like you had some luck," Joslyn said, eyeing the prisoner. "Who is he?"

"Chris Yard."

Joslyn pursed his lips, whistled soundlessly. "Whew! He's so torn up, I didn't hardly recognize him."

Yard sat slumped in the saddle, his face a mass of bruises, one eye swollen shut and the other a watery slit. He seemed oblivious to what was going on around him.

Olcott said, "What about the Hulls?"

"Still out on the trail." Joslyn chewed the corner of his mustache, anxious. "Never mind about them. We got trouble."

"Tell me later," Olcott said, urging his horse forward.

"Hey, where you going?"

"Reeb's."

Joslyn scurried alongside Olcott's horse. "Ain't you gonna lock up the prisoner?"

"Later," Olcott said. "Maybe."

"Maybe? What do you mean, maybe?"

"I might think of something better."

Joslyn faltered, stopped. Olcott pulled away. Joslyn called after him, "Wade ain't gonna like this!"

Olcott seemed undisturbed by the prospect. He kept going, with Yard in tow. The posse men exchanged glances. Two held back, the rest went with Olcott. Boyd went too. He wasn't ready to stop Olcott yet, not until he saw what the deputy was up to.

The horsemen went east on Burnett Street, then turned left on Powell, going north. Across the black flat, fire-glow showed at the mines, where the smelters were burning. Stacks vented smoke, which mingled with cloud cover to veil moon and stars.

The riders went north, crossing Mercado and Liberty, turning left on New Street. Not far from the corner, fronting the north side of the cross street, was a white wooden-framed house with black awnings. With its peaked roof, gables, dormer windows, corner turrets, and intricate architectural trimmings, it looked as if it had been transported bodily from some comfortably prosperous suburb of St. Louis. It was a two-story structure, its ground floor housing a commercial establishment, while the upper level was residential.

That is, the upper half held living quarters, while the bottom half was devoted to death. A signpost announced, in thorny Gothic lettering, that this was the site of "REEB & REEB—UNDERTAKERS."

A waist-high iron spear fence bounded the property. Olcott and company dismounted, hitching their horses to the fence. Olcott unfolded a pocketknife with a keen-edged six-inch blade and cut the bonds trying Yard to the saddle. He plucked Yard from his horse and set him down bodily. Yard's knees were weak and he would have fallen if not for Olcott's hand gripping him above the elbow, holding him up.

Indicating the house with a nod, Olcott said, "C'mon, Bowman."

"All right," Boyd said.

Olcott told his men, "Stay here. And watch out. Anything can happen."

He started up the front path to the house, sweeping Yard along with him. Yard's boot toes barely skimmed the ground. Boyd followed, up the stairs to the porch.

All the ground-floor windows sported black canvas

awnings. Lights shone dimly through heavy purple drapes. The upper floor was dark. Flanking the front door at chest height was a pair of black enameled iron sconces in the shape of winged angels holding amber globe lamps. They shed a beer-colored light.

The door was closed. Olcott knocked on it with Yard's head, banging it against the panels. No one answered. Boyd tried the handle. The door was unlocked.

Thrusting Yard before him, Olcott went through a narrow vestibule into a modest-sized front hall. On both sides were archways: The one on the right opened into a parlor; the one on the left was barred by thick purple curtains. Opposite the front door, a stairway led to the upper level. The decor featured dark wood walls, heavy furnishings, and dim lights. There was a smell compounded of sickly sweet perfume, a sharper chemical reek, and the odor of decay.

Boyd said, "Looks like nobody's home."

"Must be in the back," Olcott said.

He shoved Yard through the curtained archway on the left with such force that the curtain rings nearly tore loose from the rods.

Beyond lay a display room, walls lined with waist-high oblong platforms bearing a variety of coffins. Empty coffins. Most were simple pine boxes, but a few were made of rarer, costlier woods. At the far end of the room was a box of dark polished wood with ornate bronze handles. To the left, a door opened into a back room, the workroom.

In the center of the workroom floor, standing side by side with an aisle between them, were two tables. On them were two bodies, covered by sheets. The nearer one's hand hung down below the sheet. The sheet was dingy yellow; the hand was white, blood-less. At the tables' heads stood a smaller, square-topped table. It held saws, knives, cleavers. They hadn't been used recently, but were none too clean from their last use. In a corner of the tabletop, a chipped dinner plate held a half-eaten sandwich.

Light was supplied by an oil lamp, set on a marble-topped cabinet standing against the right-hand wall. The flame was trimmed so low that it flickered on the edge of extinction.

In the background, shelves held ten-gallon bottles of murky fluids. They gave off a sharp chemical reek. An outside door was ajar, open a few inches.

Olcott lifted a sheet off the nearest corpse, uncov-ering its head. Its identity surprised him.

"Damn! Fyfe!" he said.

Boyd was carefully blank-faced. Olcott, still holding Yard in tow, unveiled the second figure.

Olcott said, "Jess! The hell—?!"

He shook Yard, a mastiff worrying a rat. "Who killed them?"

"N-not me," Yard said, cringing. He raised a hand to protect himself. His left hand—his right arm was dead below the shoulder. He lacked the strength to raise it higher than his chest.

Olcott said, "What do you know about this, you lit-tle pissant?"

"Nothing!" Yard said.

"They were killed by your cattle-thieving pals!"

"No!"

"Who else then? Talk, damn you!"

Yard quailed. Olcott pressed: "Who was in on the stagecoach job with you? Talk!"

Yard wouldn't talk. Olcott tried to "persuade" him. Yard fainted.

"Can't take it," Olcott said, panting.

Boyd sighed. Olcott said, "If you hadn't of shot him, I could get some answers out of him without him passing out all the time."

The chemical reek tickled the back of Boyd's throat. He crossed to the back door.

Olcott said, "Where you going?"

"To get some fresh air," Boyd said.

Olcott shook his head. "I ain't letting you out of my sight."

Boyd shrugged, opening the door. "Come on then."

Yard was inert, a dead weight. Olcott held him by the collar, lifting his upper body off the floor.

"What about him?" Olcott said.

"Bring him along," Boyd said.

"He's out cold!"

"That hasn't stopped you yet."

Outside, there was the sound of hammering. A big back lot was enclosed by an eight-foot wooden plank fence. A kerosene lantern hung from the top of a pole, lighting the scene with a grimy yellow glow. At the far end of the lot was a carriage house, double doors gaping open. In the middle ground was an open space. In it was a hearse wagon and a knot of figures, standing with their heads together. They stopped talking and looked up as Boyd came out the back door.

Outside, the chemical smell was weaker, replaced by a carrion taint. The ground was bare dirt. At the edge of the light, shadows were thick, oily. Back stairs creaked under Olcott, half-carrying, half-dragging Yard. Yard's lower limbs clattered against the treads. Then a soft thud as they hit the dirt.

To the right were stacks of lumber. Straddling a workbench was a man building a coffin. Shaggy silver hair touched his shoulders. Wire-frame spectacles with tiny octagonal lenses perched on the end of a bulbous nose. His sleeves were rolled up past the elbows, baring brawny forearms. A brown leather bib apron covered his front. He was hammering nails into the side of a coffin, the wood raw and yellow-new.

He glanced at the newcomers, then ignored them, his hammering never missing a beat.

The hearse was long, tall, narrow, with a lacquered black-mirror finish. Beside it stood two men, one fat, the other, lean, both dark-clad and top-hatted. They started, then leaned forward, peering.

Boyd glanced at Olcott. "Reeb and Reeb," Olcott said, low-voiced. "Big one's Delbert, little one's Max. Foley's the coffin-maker."

Boyd nodded.

Delbert's face was spade-shaped, hairless, with thick fleshy features. His nose was a broad flat triangle. His eyes were two small triangles, points downward. He looked like a jack-o'-lantern.

"Bless my soul! It's Deputy Olcott," he said.

"Greetings, Deputy," Max intoned. His voice was deep, mournful. His features were small and neat, like a face painted on a storefront mannequin.

Foley kept at his work, saying nothing.

Dapper little Max moved forward, saying, "What

have you got for us, Deputy, another one?''

"We'll be stacking them like cordwood soon,'' Delbert muttered.

Yard stirred, groaning. Max, taken aback, said, "He's alive!''

"Sure, what else?'' Olcott said.

"I thought he was dead!''

"He's fine.''

Max was doubtful, but not inclined to press the point. Olcott said, "What's Fyfe and Jess doing in your back room?''

"Nothing. They're dead,'' Delbert said.

"I mean, who killed them?''

"Oh. That's easy. This way, please.''

Delbert entered the carriage house, the others following, all but Foley, who stayed at his post. Delbert lit a candle.

"We had to move the hearse out to make room,'' he said.

On the floor were four coffins. Three were grouped together; the fourth was set apart. Inside the three coffins were Haycox, Odell, and Clark.

"They got in a fight with Dunston's men and killed each other,'' Delbert said.

"There'll be hell to pay now,'' Olcott said, not sounding too displeased over the prospect.

He dragged Yard to the nearest coffin, Odell's. Yard was face-to-face with the corpse. Olcott said, "Your friends are dropping fast!''

Boyd went to the fourth coffin. "Who's this?''

"Osmond. Sheriff brought him in,'' Delbert said.

Olcott hefted Yard to his feet and hustled him over

to the fourth coffin. He said, "Hold that light over here, Del."

Candlelight shone down on the corpse of a big man stuffed face-up into a too-small box. His shoulders were squeezed together, so he looked like he was shrugging. There was a hole in his belly, but that wasn't what killed had him. The top of his head had been blown off at point-blank range. Not much was left above the eyebrows. Massive pressure from the wound had squeezed the face like a vise, so that it was much wider than it was long. Swollen, purple-black flesh.

Yard squinted through his one good eye at the corpse, then looked away. Olcott wouldn't let him off the hook that easily. He grabbed the bottom of Yard's face, forcing him to look at the dead man.

"Say hello to your pal," Olcott said.

Boyd said, "That's one of the robbers?"

"He was," the deputy said. "Wick Osmond. We found him at North Pass. He was hurt too bad to ride, so his pals did for him. Yard hisself here might have been the one who pulled the trigger."

"No," Yard said.

"Dead men tell no tales. But you ain't dead, Yard, not yet. Who else was in it with you?"

Yard clamped his jaws shut, shook his head.

"Still won't talk," Olcott said. "You want to hang while the others go free. I can guess one, though: Ricky Ray Prewitt. It was Ricky Ray, wasn't it? Shoot, don't try to deny it, boy. You and Wick and Prewitt was a team, everybody knows that. Now,

Wick's dead, you're gallows-bait, and Ricky Ray's running free and clear.''

"No.'' Yard spoke through clenched teeth.

"No, it wasn't Ricky Ray, or no, you didn't do it?''

"Both.''

Olcott laughed. "I know it was him and I know it was you. What I don't know is who the fourth man was. I will, but I don't yet. You could save me some time and yourself a whole lot of grief by telling me.''

Yard was stubborn, unyielding. Boyd said, "He won't talk.''

"He'll talk,'' Olcott said. His jaws worked as he tightened his grip on Yard. Yard flinched, anticipating pain.

Max Reeb stepped in.

"Please, Deputy, no unpleasantness. Out of respect for the dead,'' he said.

"Them sumbitches never had any respect for the living,'' Olcott said, but he held his hand.

Boyd said, "Your friends are liable to give you the same treatment as Osmond, Yard.''

"I'd like to see that,'' the deputy said. "By God, I surely would like to see them try.''

Yard croaked, "You got the wrong man. I'm innocent.''

He fainted.

"Here we go again,'' Olcott said cheerfully.

Boyd said, "Better wait before you start in on him. He can't take much more.''

Olcott thought about it, nodded. "I can wait. He ain't going nowhere—'cept to jail, that is.''

Max shuffled impatiently. "If you're through, Deputy, we've still got our work to do."

Boyd said, "When's the funeral?"

"Tomorrow," Delbert said.

"And Dunston's men?"

"Them too. They'll be buried in the morning; these others, in the afternoon," Delbert said.

Max nodded. "It wouldn't do to have both sets of funerals at the same time. Feelings will be running high among the mourners."

Boyd said, "Who's paying to bury the rustlers?"

"Mr. Parry, I assume. The deceased were his friends," Max said.

"Is he in town now?"

"Not that I know of."

Delbert said, "Not yet."

Olcott collared Yard. "Time this one was locked up."

"You might as well leave him here. There's not a whole lot of him left," Boyd said.

"Yeah, he looks pretty bad," Olcott agreed. "I'll get Doc Grinnell to patch him up, soon as he 'fesses up about who his accomplices is."

He leaned down, sticking his face in Yard's. "How 'bout it, boy? You ready to talk?"

"I think he's still unconscious," Boyd said.

"Huh? Well, mebbe so, mebbe so," the deputy said.

He exited the carriage house, dragging Yard through the dirt. The others followed, Delbert pausing to blow out the candle.

A voice hailed Olcott, as a posse man rounded the corner of the house, coming into view.

"Another one," the posse man said.

"Another one *what*?" Olcott said.

"Another body."

Up the drive came a two-horse team, plodding, drawing a freight wagon. The driver was clean-shaven, sharp-featured. Beside him sat Hardrock Riley, Mine Boss Seaton's man.

The wagon stopped. Riley got down, went around to the back of the wagon, and lowered the gate. In the bed lay a blanket-covered body.

Olcott said, "Who's that?"

"Joe Craigie," Riley said.

"Craigie! The missing guard!" the posse man said.

"He ain't missing no more" Riley said. "We found him at the bottom of an abandoned shaft. He'd been knifed."

"From the front or behind?" Boyd asked.

"From the front," Riley said.

"Ripped him right up the belly," the driver said, smacking his lips, as though relishing the details.

Riley frowned, regretting having answered. He stared at Boyd. "What's it to you, mister? And who are you anyhow?"

Olcott stepped in. "He's working with me, Riley, helping out the law."

"That LaRue's idea? Or yours?"

"Never mind about that. It's every citizen's duty to help out the law."

"You'll need all the help you can get. I hear Jeff Parry's coming in."

"Let him come. I got no quarrel with him."

"No? Maybe he'll think different when he sees how

you done Yard,'' Riley said.

The driver started, staring at the prisoner.

''Is that Yard? Chris Yard? Man, you sure whomped crap out of him!'' he said.

''Yeah. He wasn't cooperating,'' Olcott said dryly.

He turned to the undertakers. ''Don't do nothing with the body till Grinnell's seen it.''

''We won't,'' Delbert said.

''We won't be able to get to it for hours yet anyway, we're so busy,'' Max said.

Olcott began, ''I got me an idea, Bowman.''

He stopped, realizing he was speaking to empty air. Boyd was gone.

Seven

Jeff Parry wore a ten-gallon hat and three guns. The hat was tan, well-worn, its brim turned up so the edges touched the crown. Two of the guns were in side holsters; the third was in a gunbelt looped across his shoulder, weapon holstered butt-out under his left arm. He was heavyset, fortyish, shaggy-haired—coarse black hair, shot through with gray. His brows were pointed in the middle. An old scar curled out of the corner of his upper lip, giving him a wolfish mouth. He wore a brown leather vest, a red-and-black plaid flannel shirt, brown leather chaps over jeans. His spurs had oversized silver sunburst rowels.

He sat on a horse in Mercado Street, outside the Majestic Hotel. With him were eight riders, members of the gang. Boyd recognized some of them, from their likenesses on wanted circulars and Cattleman's Protective Association confidential reports.

At Parry's side was the gunfighter called Concho, fastest draw in the gang, maybe in the territory. His low-crowned, wide-brimmed black hat had a hat band of tiny silver shells with turquoise centers. A black leather gun-belt was studded with larger versions of those same silver shells. The man had deep-set, feverish eyes in a blank, immobile face.

Also present was Chet Buckhorn, filthy and foul-mouthed, native to the plateau; Drury Lake, handsome, reckless; Trey Rollin, the cowboy card shark; O.C. "Easy" Stemple, from Mt. Pisgah, Colorado; Hector Martinez, twenty-three, reputed to have killed twenty-six men in Mexico before fleeing north of the border; and three others, unknown to Boyd. All well-armed, on good horses.

Boyd had just come from the livery stable, where the gray was bedded down for the night. He was walking west on the north side of Mercado, about a block away from the hotel, when Parry came.

The arrival was quiet, undramatic. Instead of riding in at a gallop, hell-bent-for-leather, the gang drifted in cool and easy. They were almost in front of the hotel before anybody took notice.

Jeff Parry said, *"Dunston!"*

He was loud, leather-lunged. Passersby started running, taking cover. Boyd ducked halfway into a recessed doorway.

Parry took a deep breath and bawled Dunston's name again, calling him out. The gang was bunched up in front of the hotel. Boyd regretted not being on a rooftop with dynamite and a Winchester. That would clean up most of his problems.

LaRue came out of the hotel, all duded up in a tan

suit with a brown vest, and a tan hat with a brown hat band. He wore a side-gun and, on his lapel, a badge.

Concho said, "You ain't Dunston." He spoke in a monotone.

Ignoring him, LaRue spoke to Parry. "Hello, Jeff."

"Wade," Parry said.

"What do you want, Jeff?"

"Dunston."

"What do you want him for?"

"Murder."

LaRue shook his head. "You know that's not so, Jeff."

"He killed three men. My men."

"Two of his are dead too."

"What's that to me?"

"They all killed each other. It's over."

"Not to me," Parry said.

Chet Buckhorn spat. He had long, dirty silver hair and beard, and wore rank buckskins. He said, "Cut the bullshit and give us Dunston!"

LaRue said mildly, "He speaking for you, Jeff?"

"No."

"Glad to hear it." LaRue smiled, turned toward Buckhorn. "Get down off that horse, Chet."

"Like hell!" Buckhorn said.

LaRue squared his stance and swept his jacket flap back over his gun, out of the way. "Get down, Chet."

Buckhorn laughed. "You gonna take us all on, Sheriff?"

"No, just you," Parry said.

Buckhorn started, his bluster deflating. "Quit funning, Jeff."

"I said you didn't speak for me. Wade's a friend of mine. You're on your own," Parry said. "You hear that, the rest of you?"

The others heard. Those nearest Buckhorn moved away.

LaRue said, "Get off your horse. I won't tell you again."

Buckhorn chewed his lips, darting nervous glances. *"Jeff!"*

Parry shook his head. Concho said, "Draw or crawl, Buckhorn."

Buckhorn was rigid, corded with tension. Parry let him hang fire for long seconds.

"Course, being a friend, Wade might be inclined to let you go, if I asked him," Jeff drawled.

"You asking?" LaRue said.

"I'd appreciate it if you didn't kill him. I've already got too many men dead today."

"Anything for a friend."

"Much obliged, Wade."

LaRue said, "Buckhorn, the next time you talk out of turn, be ready to tangle."

Buckhorn opened his mouth to speak. Parry said, "Shut up." Buckhorn's jaws closed with an audible click.

"He thanks you too," Parry said.

LaRue nodded. Parry said, "Let's go, men."

Easy Stemple, jug-eared and red-faced, said, "What about Dunston?"

"He ain't here," Concho said.

"What!"

"Sure," Jeff Parry said, chuckling. "One thing I'll

give that old son of a bitch, he's not afraid to mix it up. If he was here, he'd of come out shooting by now.''

LaRue said, ''I asked him to go home, to keep the peace.''

''Right smart of you, Wade. What are you fixing to do about him?''

''Well, now, Jeff, I can't see where there's a whole lot I can do. Your men were killed on Dunston land, but not before they killed their killers. What they were doing there, I couldn't say, but the fact is that their lives were forfeit when they crossed the line into Dunston's land. That's the law. If Fyfe and Jess had lived, I couldn't have charged them with anything. But if your men lived, I'd have had to charge them with murder.''

''So you won't do anything.''

''I can't.''

''I don't blame you for not wanting to buck Dunston, Wade. He's a big man.''

''That's not it. It's the law.''

''Since when did you become such an all-fired stickler for the law?'' Parry said.

Concho said, ''It's an election year.''

''So what? Dunston ain't backing Wade anyhow. He's backing Oates Hull for sheriff. Wade ain't good enough for him.''

LaRue said, ''You won't like it so well either if Hull gets elected.''

''Yeah, well, Dunston killed three votes for you. Think on that, Sheriff,'' Parry said.

''Four, counting Wick Osmond. He's dead too.''

''So?''

"He died trying to rob a stagecoach. He used to ride with you."

Parry smiled tolerantly. "He used to hang around at Rock House. That's not the same as riding with me. Besides, you're barking up the wrong tree. If you want to know about the holdup, ask the marshal."

"What?"

"Oates Hull. He knows. Ask him."

"I'm asking you, Jeff."

"I don't know nothing about no holdups, Wade. Dunston's my concern. You stick to your business and I'll stick to mine."

"Keeping the peace is my business."

"Ask Hull about the holdups, Wade."

"I will."

"See you," Parry said.

He rode away, his men following. They passed Boyd, giving him not so much as a second glance. Buckhorn was saying, "You shouldn't have done me like that, Jeff. That wasn't right."

"I warned you about that big mouth. I don't need you to go picking fights with the sheriff, not now," Parry said.

"I could have taken him."

Concho snorted. Parry said something in reply, but he was too far out of earshot for Boyd to make it out.

Dust kicked up in their wake hung over the street after the gang was gone. They didn't go far, only to the saloons on East Burnett Street, near the jail.

LaRue stood with his hands on his hips, watching them go. He gave his head a little shake and went back inside.

Boyd lit up a smoke and thought things over. He flipped the stub in the street and went into the hotel.

The lobby of the Majestic was bright, after the outdoors. Good food smells drifted in from the dining room. Boyd's stomach rumbled. He was hot, hungry, tired, and dirty.

Off in a corner, partly shielded by a potted plant, were LaRue and Clarissa Bane. They stood facing each other, LaRue holding her arms. The redhead's body was angular with fear, no mean feat considering her well-rounded curves. Her face was pale, eyes wide. LaRue was trying to calm her. They spoke in low, earnest tones.

Clarissa stiffened as Boyd approached. LaRue eyed him, wary, appraising. He subtly managed to turn Clarissa so he stood between her and the newcomer.

LaRue said, "Something I can do for you, Mr., ah, Bowman, wasn't it?"

Boyd nodded. "Olcott's looking for you, Sheriff. He's got a prisoner. One of the stage robbers."

"Who?"

"Fellow name of Yard."

"Chris Yard? One of the Rock House crowd?"

Boyd shrugged, implying the matter meant little to him. "I don't know about any Rock House, but Chris Yard, yeah, that's the man."

"Hmmm." LaRue fingered the corners of his mustache, looking as if he were unsure whether to be pleased or worried.

He said, "Where's Olcott now?"

"Over to the undertaker's, last I saw him," Boyd said.

"Thanks. Much obliged." LaRue looked up and down at Boyd. "You've been doing some hard riding, Bowman."

"Hard country, Sheriff."

"And dangerous, to those who don't know their way around."

"I'll take my chances. See you," Boyd said. He touched his hat, nodding toward Clarissa. "Ma'am . . ."

He turned, crossing toward the desk. He heard LaRue and Clarissa conversing intently behind him.

Weaver manned the front desk. The dapper little man seemed preoccupied, but he greeted Boyd with professional good cheer.

"Good evening, Mr. Bowman. Glad to have you back with us."

"Glad to be back. Did you save my room?"

"As per your instructions."

"Thanks. Can I get a bath, a hot bath?"

"Yes, sir. When would you like it?"

"Now," Boyd said.

Weaver tapped the bell, summoning a bellboy, the rheumy, white-haired old "boy," giving him his instructions. The underling shuffled away.

Weaver fished out an envelope from a pile of papers on his desk. "This came for you."

Boyd took it, unsealed it. Inside was a telegram, addressed to "Bowman," care of the hotel.

It said:

ST LOUIS
BULL OF THE WOODS ACTING UP STOP SUS-

PECT SECRET DEAL WITH THIRD PARTY TO
SOLVE PROBLEM STOP RIVAL SALESMAN MAY-
FIELD REPUTED RED-HOT STOP HOPING FOR
A SWIFT SAFE RESOLUTION

(signed)

HERMAN O'GRADY
TERMINUS MFG CO
[END]

Boyd read between the lines to get the message. The
sender was his brother, Warren McMasters, twelve years
his senior, president of the Cattleman's Protective Association. "Herman O'Grandy" was *hermano grande*—
Spanish for "big brother." His office, and Association
headquarters, was a three-story building on Enid Street
in Oklahoma City, near the railroad depot. Warren had
arranged for messages to be routed through St. Louis, to
cover Boyd's tracks. Boyd had no doubt that there really
was a Terminus Wire Fence Manufacturing Company in
St. Louis, if only an office near the telegraph station
where inquiries could be received and rerouted. Warren
had studied the Pinkertons and adopted some of their
methods. He was always after Boyd to cipher his messages and send them in code, but Boyd couldn't be bothered with such foolishness. So they'd worked out a
private code of their own, simple, easy to remember.

"Bull of the Woods" was Dunston. The Association's
biggest member in these parts, he threw plenty of
weight. He must be throwing some of it around now, to
judge by the telegram. Warren was a fiercely independent cuss, well-respected, secure in his post, but a man
like Dunston could exert a lot of pressure. Warren could
handle that. That wasn't why he'd contacted Boyd. He

wouldn't have bothered his younger brother with his troubles. Rather, his purpose was to alert Boyd that Dunston had brought a new factor into play, a third party. "SALESMAN MAYFIELD REPUTED RED-HOT." "Salesman" meant gunman; "red-hot" meant what it said.

Boyd already knew about Mayfield, but Warren hadn't known that when he sent the telegram. Gunfighter Mayfield complicated a volatile situation. Having him on your side was the next worst thing to going against him. And with Dunston as his patron . . . Dunston was hard, high-handed, a trampler. The majority of complaints from Five Creeks rancher-members to the Association concerned Parry's gang of rustlers. Running a close second were complaints about Dunston's outfit, for tearing down fences, grazing herds on other men's land, rounding up neighbors' unmarked calves, arbitrarily withholding and denying water rights, etc., etc.

Those two hanged men, Byers and DePugh, might come in handy yet. They were Boyd's hole card . . . not the only one.

Boyd folded the telegram and pocketed it. "I want to send a reply. Is the telegraph office still open?"

"Yes, sir," Weaver said. "Write your message here and I'll have a boy run it over for you."

He supplied Boyd with pencil and paper. Boyd addressed it to the St. Louis location.

Weaver busied himself at the far end of the desk.

Boyd wrote:

EXPECT TO FINISH BUSINESS HERE IN
24 HOURS

(signed)

BOWMAN

He folded the message, putting it in an envelope which Weaver had provided. He gave it to Weaver.

Weaver said, "It's not sealed."

"I'm an open book," said Boyd.

A kitchen boy was pressed into service for the errand. Boyd gave him money for the telegram and something for his trouble. The boy took off at a run.

Boyd looked around. LaRue was gone. Clarissa, alone, climbed the stairs, vanishing somewhere on the second floor.

Adroit questioning elicited the information from Weaver that no one resembling Mayfield's description had been seen in the hotel today—or in town, as far as Weaver knew.

Boyd went upstairs to his room. It seemed undisturbed. The layer of red dust from the smelter that had drifted through the open window and settled on sill and floor was untouched. Boyd ripped up the telegram into tiny pieces and dropped them out the window, a flurry of paper snow. He exited the room, a bundle of clean clothing under his arm.

The washroom was on the ground floor, in the back near the kitchen, where the water was heated. The wizened bellboy ushered Boyd into a small square room with a tall ceiling. A galvanized steel tub sat on a wooden platform, six inches tall. The tub was filled with hot water. Steam rose from it, fogging the slitlike window set high in the wall.

Boyd gave the bellman a coin. He'd been passing out
a lot of coins lately. That was living in a hotel for you.
The bellman mumbled thanks, exiting with a promise to
bring more hot water.

Boyd stripped. He was long, sinewy, and pale except for
his weathered face and hands. He slipped a gun inside a
folded towel, setting it down on a bench beside the tub. The
gun, within easy reach, was pointed at the door.

He stepped into the tub, wincing at the heat. It was
too hot to sit in, so he stood there for a minute, getting
used to it. When he finally sat down, the water went
from clear to gray. The heat soaked into his trail-weary
bones, soothing them. . . .

A knock on the door. "Come in," Boyd said.

It was Holly, the young blond lovely he'd seen waiting tables in the hotel dining room. She lugged a steaming pail, handle held in both hands.

"I brought your hot water," she said.

When he was sure that she was alone, with no one
lurking outside in the hall, he eased his hand out from
under the towel, where it had been holding his gun.

"Hello," he said. "Excuse me for not standing up
when a lady enters the room."

"You've got nothing I ain't seen before, mister," she
said.

"No? Then what're you doing here?"

"To fetch your hot water. Ol' Reg had to lie down
and rest after filling the tub."

Tendrils of steam curled out the doorway, into the
hall. Boyd said, "You left the door open."

"It ain't proper for a man and woman to be alone in
a room together, less'n the door is open," she said. "Be-

sides, Mr. Weaver wouldn't like it.''

She set the pail down on the platform at the foot of the tub. Her face was moist, flushed with the steam. She straightened up, brushing a strand of blond hair off her forehead with the back of her hand.

She said, ''You can pour the water yourself. This is as close as I get. Some men get a little too grabby.''

''Um,'' Boyd said. ''Well, thanks.''

She turned, started for the door. He called after her. ''I'd give you something for your trouble, but as you can see, I don't have any ready coin to hand. I'll take care of you later.''

She paused at the door, looking back over her shoulder.

''For the right price, I'll take care of you.''

''What would Mr. Weaver say about that?''

''Not a damn thing,'' she said. ''What I do on my off hours is my business. Besides, I won't tell ... will you?''

''I've got some business to take care of tonight myself,'' Boyd said. ''Some other time maybe.''

''Sounds like you're running out of steam, mister,'' she said.

She went out, closing the door behind her. Hard. Boyd frowned, then broke into a laugh, a harsh cawing sound that grated on his ears. He was out of practice. There hadn't been much to laugh about in the last year or so.

The aftereffects of the girl's presence made his blood sing. He had a woman, a good woman, Martha by name. But she was back home and he was here. A fierce physical urge stirred in him, a hunger of the flesh. Holly was pretty and available. What's more, he liked her, liked her spunk. He'd do her a favor and stay away from her. Being around him could be dangerous, even fatal. It had been before. . . .

Later, washed, shaved, and wearing clean clothes, he went back to his room. His dirty clothes went into a corner of his carpetbag. They needed laundering, but he didn't know how long he'd be in town. He might have to leave at the drop of a hat.

The gun he had fired, he cleaned and oiled. The other gun, he wiped clean of dust, and ran a cotton swab down the bore. His movements were neat, precise, orderly. The routine with the ramrod, swatches, and wire-bristle brushes steadied, centered him. The gun oil had a pleasant scent.

He put the cleaning kit away, donned his guns, and went down to dinner.

The dining room was about half-full, with many of those seated finishing up their meals. Boyd didn't see anybody he didn't want to see, so he went in.

Standing near the entrance was Delores. Her dress was the color of burgundy wine. She wore a necklace of gold coins strung together, and heavy gold bracelets. Her gaze was turned on the room but her thoughts seemed elsewhere.

"Hello," Boyd said.

She nodded, that was all.

He took a side table, away from any windows. He sat with his back to the wall, with a clear sightline of the room. No one could enter from the front or from the kitchen without his knowing it.

Holly served him. A white bib apron was tied around her front, confining her high pert breasts. Boyd was famished. A thick steak, 'taters, and greens, washed down with mugs of sweet cider, slaked his appetite. Slowing down, he polished off two pieces of pie and a quart of hot black coffee.

During the meal, he watched Delores. She was watching for someone else, judging by the frequent glances she cast at the lobby. As time passed, with no sign of whomever she was seeking, her expression set, became grimmer. A pair of vertical creases appeared between her brows. Her eyes flashed. Veins stood out on her neck and temples. Apart from these signs of stress, she betrayed no emotion. Her face was a bronze mask.

The dinner crowd had thinned out, with only a handful of stragglers left at the tables. Delores crossed to the entryway, soft black leather ankle boots showing under the hem of her dress, heels clicking on the floorboards in irritable staccato rhythms. She stood under the archway, hands on hips, peering into the lobby. Her body, vibrant with tension, was outlined under her dress. She held the pose for half a minute. Apparently the object of her interest was nowhere in sight, for she gave her head a short, angry shake and turned away. Reentering the dining room, she performed, perhaps unconsciously, a washing gesture with her hands. Her chin was high and her shoulders straight. She caught Boyd eyeing her. He nodded. She flashed him a dark glance that could have meant many things, then went behind a counter where she busied herself with some receipts.

"Careful you don't get burned," Holly said.

She had come up alongside Boyd, holding a steaming pot of coffee. She said, "Want some?"

"What, coffee?" Boyd said.

"Sure, what did you think I meant?"

Boyd let that pass. His cup was down to the dregs. He slid cup and saucer across the table toward Holly, saying, "Please."

She refilled the cup. "Thanks," Boyd said.

"You're welcome. In a lower voice, half-amused, half-irked, she said, "What're you interested in her for?"

"Who?" Boyd said innocently.

"Butter wouldn't melt in your mouth! You know who: Miss Delores."

"Why would any man be interested in her?"

"You ain't that backward, cowboy. Or maybe you are, if you think you can get anywhere with her."

"Why not?"

"Too rich for your blood. You've got to have the gold to go with her," Holly said.

She stood with her back to Delores, who in any case took little note of her surroundings.

"Better not let her catch you standing around," Boyd said. "She don't seem to be in too good a mood tonight."

"Or any other night," Holly said. She made herself look busy, flicking crumbs off the table, straightening the tablecloth.

Under her breath, she said, "She's never easy, but the last few days she's been a regular terror!"

"Right about the time that I hit town. Well, I do have that effect on women."

Holly rolled her eyes to heaven. "Listen to him!"

"I don't have that effect on you, Holly?"

"Now, you're just funning with me. I don't mind. But

let me tell you something: Miss Delores don't give a snap for you, or any other man, so far as I can tell.

"And I could tell plenty," she added, reaching for his dessert plate.

"Not so fast," he said.

"Ain't you done yet? You already had two pieces of pie."

"Believe I'll have a third. I've got a sweet tooth."

"Yeah, I can see you sitting there with your mouth watering," Holly said.

She whisked away into the kitchen.

Into the dining room came Doug Seaton. The mine boss was grim, intent. His steps faltered when he saw Delores, but only for an instant. He changed course and bore down on her. She kept her eyes on her paperwork, not raising them, but she had been aware of his presence from the start. A stiffness in her posture told that.

He faced her across the counter. After a deliberate pause, she looked up, staring him in the face. He leaned forward, hands on the edge of the countertop. He exchanged words with Delores. Boyd was too far away to hear what they were. Seaton did most of the talking. Delores's replies were quick, curt. Seaton leaned far forward over the counter, thrusting his face close to hers. He gave the impression of a man fighting a losing battle to control his temper. He might as well have been talking to the wall, for all the encouragement she gave him.

Holly set down a fresh piece of pie in front of Boyd. "Mmmmm," Boyd said.

"Don't bite off more than you can chew," she said. "You might choke on it."

Without delay, she vanished into the kitchen. She

could read the storm signals well enough and had decided to make herself scarce.

Seaton was pressing his argument, whatever it was.
His voice rose. He glanced over his shoulder to see if
anyone was listening. Boyd's gaze was fastened on the
pie, as he solemnly subtracted a forkful.

Delores, stony-faced, folded her arms across her chest.
Seaton kept on talking, loud, blustering. When he paused
for breath, she got her line in. Whatever she had said, it
stopped him short. His face darkened, jaws working. He
spat out a reply. Delores reeled, as if struck in the face.
She recovered almost immediately, drawing herself up,
a mirthless smile playing around her lips.

Latent violence hung in the air. Boyd sat frozen, fork
suspended midway between plate and mouth.

Abruptly, Delores came out from behind the counter
and started to walk away. Seaton called her name, to no
avail. He didn't like being ignored. He started after her,
grabbed her by the wrist. She tried to pull free, but was
unable to break his grip. He smirked. She raised the hand
to her mouth and sank her teeth into it, drawing blood.
He cried out, cursed, let go.

He raised a hand to strike her. She moved faster. She
reached into the folds of her skirt, and suddenly
something sharp and bright flashed into her hand. A
knife. A lady's dagger, slim, elegant. Its point gleamed
a few inches short of Seaton's belly.

He checked his swing, froze. Sucked in his belly, hol-
lowing it to put a few more precious inches between
him and the blade. Delores held the knife as if she knew
how to use it. Indeed, she looked like her fondest wish
was to bury it in his soft parts and start carving.

Seaton stepped back, turned, and stormed from the room. He nearly collided with the ancient bellman, who stood hunched under the archway. The oldster lurched aside, forestalling a crash. He staggered, fighting for balance while Seaton crossed the lobby and went out the front entrance.

When Boyd looked again, Delores was empty-handed, having made the knife disappear with the same mysterious sleight of hand she had used to materialize it.

Boyd pushed back his chair and stood up, leaving his pie half-eaten. He threw some money down on the table, payment for the bill with something left over for Holly.

It would be instructive to see what Seaton would do next. Boyd made for the exit. As he drew abreast of the front desk, he was hailed by Weaver.

"They weren't able to send your telegram, Mr. Bowman. The lines must be down," Weaver said.

"That so? How long have they been down?"

"They were working fine this afternoon. Odd. Every now and then, a storm will put the telegraph out of commission, but it hasn't so much as rained today."

"These things happen. Tell 'em to send the message when they can, please."

"Yessir, Mr. Bowman."

Boyd went out on the verandah, sidling into the shadows. The street was alive with lights, motion, people. It was livelier at night than during the day. It reminded Boyd of a county fair.

The air was thick, close, oppressive. Low clouds covered the sky, seeming to graze the rooftops. A breeze rose, tugging at Boyd's garments. It grew, picking up dirt, scouring the street with wind-borne chaff. Curtains lifted, billowing; windows rattled in their frames. Boyd clapped a hand on his hat to keep from losing it. Others, not so quick, lost theirs, hats cartwheeling away into darkness.

The wind fell away. People laughed, buzzed, went about their business. Boyd stood in the lee of a porch column, lighting a long black cigar. After he got it going, he set about on his business.

Eight

Kip Kingston asked, "This yours?"

He held out a hat to Boyd, who took it. It was battered, sun-bleached, and weathered.

"That's mine, all right," Boyd said. "Much obliged, Mr. . . . ?"

"Kingston. Kip Kingston. And you're Bowman."

"That's right."

"Glad to know you," Kip said.

They shook hands. Boyd said, "Let me buy you a drink."

"Don't mind if I do."

Boyd sat at a table in the Beacon Saloon. The saloon fronted the east side of Grand Street, at the corner of Grand and Liberty. The building was a barnlike structure with its long sides running east-west. As one entered through the front double-swinging doors, there was a long bar on the right. At the opposite end was a small stage, now empty. To the right of the stage, a staircase led to the second floor, where there were a number of private rooms. A balcony jutted out from the rear wall, above the stage, making a right-angle turn to stretch the length of the long left wall.

Boyd's table was under the balcony, at about the midpoint of the long wall. He sat with his back to the wall, with a clear sightline of the entrance and the rear staircase. Kingston pulled up a chair, placing it so that he too enjoyed similar advantages.

It was about ten o'clock at night. The saloon was booming. Men were lined up at the bar, and the tables were filled. In the center of the floor were games of chance: faro, a roulette wheel, card tables. All were filled to capacity. The air was thick with smoke, sweat, whiskey fumes, the smell of stale beer, and sawdust. Waves of noise rose and fell, echoing and reechoing in the cavernous high-ceilinged space. Serving girls circulated through the crowd with trays of drinks, stepping lively to dodge lewd clutching hands.

Kingston caught the eye of one of the girls. A moment later, she returned with a bottle of whiskey and two tumblers. As she set them down on the table, Boyd reached into his pocket for some money.

"It's all taken care of," Kingston said.

"Can't let the lady go away without something for her trouble," Boyd said.

He put a coin on the table. The serving girl swooped it up and made it disappear, favoring Boyd with a wink as she flounced away.

Kingston cracked the seal on the bottle, poured two drinks. "Here's how," he said, raising his glass.

Boyd nodded. An instant later, two empty glasses

were set down on the tabletop.

"Good stuff," Boyd said.

"Private stock. I'm like one of the family here," Kingston said.

While he poured a refill, Boyd changed hats. He punched his old one into shape, creasing the brim the way he liked it.

"I didn't expect to see this again," he said.

"I found it out at North Pass," Kingston said.

"Like I said, much obliged. It ain't much, but I'm used to it. That new hat just didn't cut it."

They drank some more. The whiskey was liquid fire. Boyd welcomed it. The weight of dinner had slowed him down; this would quicken him up.

Kingston said, "How do you like Smoke Tree?"

Boyd shrugged. "I'm not much of a townman."

"Lot of opportunities. Good cattle country hereabouts."

"Plenty of rustlers too, I hear."

"That's no lie," Kingston said.

He resembled the Hulls, with his rawboned face, thick mustache, and townman's dark suit of clothes. But where their eyes were blue, his were green, and his features were sharper, more hawklike.

He said, "That was some nice shooting you did."

Boyd looked at him.

"Osmond, the stagecoach robber," Kingston said.

"Lucky shot."

"At that distance? With a pistol, at night? Friend, I'd call that more than luck."

"He was still alive after I shot him. I heard him yelling."

"Gut-shot. His partners finished him off."

"What are friends for?"

"Ha, ha," Kingston said. "Still, you might want to keep that in mind."

"Why?"

"Well, two of the robbers are still loose."

"You think they might come after me?"

"You spoiled their chance for a big payday."

"They'd do better to go after the gold," Boyd said.

Kingston refilled his glass. He reached to pour some more for Boyd, who declined, saying, "I'm fine, thanks."

Kingston held his glass in both hands, not drinking from it. "That payroll gold's blown up."

"Could be," Boyd said.

He sipped some whiskey, holding it in his mouth, letting it burn on his tongue.

"Anyhow, gold's not what I'm after," Boyd said.

Kingston leaned forward. "Just what are you after, Bowman?"

"Livestock. Let the law find out who got the gold, if there's any gold to be got. It's nothing to me."

Kingston smiled his disbelief. "You saying you don't like gold?"

"Not at this price. Three men dead: Randle, the shotgun messenger; Osmond; and Craigie, the mine guard. And how many more? No, I'll stick to my line. It's safer."

"You might have something there," Kingston allowed. "Why go messing in something that's not your affair?"

"Them's my thoughts."

"Let's drink on it."

They drank. Kingston was red-faced, glitter-eyed; Boyd, much the same. Both sets of eyes were in restless, constant motion, scanning the surroundings. Kingston's gaze fastened on the front of the saloon and stayed there. The corners of his lips quirked upward. He let out a soft sigh, as if sinking into a warm bath.

Boyd turned his attention in the same direction. Three men had just come into the saloon, the double doors swinging behind them. Tough-looking hombres who showed signs of hard riding. Their hats were pulled down and their gunbelts worn low. Those nearest to them sidled out of the way, but the crowd was too big and boisterous for the newcomers to have made much of an impression.

They saw Kingston and made a beeline for his table.

"Friends of yours?" Boyd said.

"I've got lots of friends," Kingston said.

"They don't look too friendly."

"See that fellow in the middle, the tall shaggy one? That's Clete Skraggs. His partner was Osmond, the man you shot. Funny, huh?"

"I'm busting a gut," Boyd said.

"The one on his left is Panamint, and the other one's Nacker," Kingston said.

Skraggs was tall, hollow-cheeked, with hot eyes in deep sockets. Panamint was short, with a square-shaped face and square high-waisted torso. Nacker was bow-legged, with long lank strands of mouse-brown hair falling in front of his face. He kept tossing his head to get the hair out of his eyes, only to have it immediately fall back into the same place.

They halted on the other side of the table. Skraggs leaned forward, hands on his gun butts.

He said, "I ben lookin' fer yew, Kingston."

"You found me, Clete."

"Surprised to see me, eh?"

"I figured you'd be a long way off from here, since you're wanted for that stagecoach holdup."

"Not no more," Skraggs said.

Panamint said, "Clete's got a clean bill of health. A dozen witnesses swore he was miles away when that robbery took place."

"All Rock House boys, I'm sure," Kingston said.

"I reckon our word's as good as anyone else's, and better than most," Panamint said.

"As good as Chris Yard's?"

"What about him, Kingston?"

"He's sitting in LaRue's jail."

"A dozen witnesses will swear that he was at Rock House too," Panamint said.

Kingston sat easily, with both hands folded on the table.

"So?" he said.

Skraggs said, "I wanted to let yew know I was in town. We got us some unfinished business, Kingston."

"We can finish it now, if you like."

"We'll finish it—"

Panamint said quickly, warningly, *"Clete!"*

"But not yet," Skraggs said. "Yew can twist around on the end of a rope a while longer."

"We'll finish it now."

"Feel that noose a-tightenin' already, Kingston?"

"I'm not going to wait around for you to shoot me in the back."

"When I shoot yew, I'll be lookin' yew straight in the eye!"

"Now you're talking," Kingston said.

Panamint said, "Jeff said no shooting, Clete!"

"I heerd him," Skraggs said. His hands were in the air, away from his guns. "Kingston won't shoot an unarmed man—not in front of witnesses anyhow."

"You said your say. Let's go," Panamint said to Skraggs.

Kingston said, "Scared, Clete?"

"Of you? Pshaw!"

"Then why turn tail and run away like a yellow dog?"

Panamint said, "He's trying to rile you, Clete."

"I know what he's tryin' to do, I ain't stupid."

"No?" Kingston said.

"Save your breath, I'm rile-proof. Ain't much fun a-danglin' on that rope, is it, Kingston? Poor ol' Wick Osmond didn't know what hit him, but yew'll have plenty of time to think about what's coming," Skraggs said.

Skraggs and Panamint turned to leave, but Nacker lingered. He stared Boyd in the face, as he had been doing for some time since the start of the confrontation. Slitted eyes peered out from behind rat-tail strands of hair with dawning recognition.

Panamint tapped Nacker on the shoulder, saying, "C'mon."

"I know you," Nacker said.

Boyd was silent.

Panamint said, "Nacker . . ."

"I know him. I know him!"

"Some other time," Panamint said. He grasped Nacker's upper arm to lead him away, but Nacker was immobile.

"McMasters! That's who you are," Nacker said.

Kingston, eyes hooded, said, "Wrong man, friend. This fellow's named Bowman."

"Like hell!"

Panamint, irritated, said, "McMasters, Bowman, who cares?"

"I do! And if you're smart, you will too!"

"What are you trying to pull, Nacker?!"

Nacker shook off the other's restraining hand. "Listen! You know who heads the Cattleman's Protective Association? *McMasters!*"

"Him? Sitting there at that table?"

"Not him, his brother!"

Panamint laughed uneasily. "You're loco, Nacker."

"That's Boyd McMasters! His brother heads the Association, but this one does the dirty work."

Panamint said, "Funny company you keep, Kingston. Looks like you've been crossing everybody right along."

"It's news to me," Kingston said. "I thought he was Bowman, a cattle buyer. Why would I get mixed up with the Association?"

"Why indeed? Maybe because it's a way to get shut of some old pards you've grown too big for. But that cuts two ways, Kingston. You of all people might want to keep that in mind."

"How do you know he's Association? Just because

Nacker says it's so, don't mean it's so.'' Kingston put
plenty of contempt into the word "Nacker."

Panamint must have been uncertain of Nacker's cred-
ibility, for he demanded, "You sure, Nacker?"

"Hell, yes! Think I'd forget him?" Nacker stabbed a
pointing forefinger at Boyd, who didn't so much as
blink.

"He used to be sheriff of Reeves County, Texas, till
he murdered a whole family, womenfolk and all! He was
such a good killer that his brother made him the Association's top gun!" Nacker said.

Kingston's eyebrows lifted. He said mildly, "You're
full of surprises, Bowman—or is that McMasters?"

"It's McMasters," Boyd said.

Skraggs shoved his face forward. "We don't rightly
care for your kind in these parts, Mr. Association Man!
That fellow Bland was snoopin' around and look where
it got him!"

"A bullet in the back," Boyd said.

"That's right!"

"What do you know about that?"

Before Skraggs could reply, Panamint said sharply,
"Shut up, Clete. You've said enough. Let's get out of
here. Jeff will want to know about this."

Skraggs was ready to go, but Nacker had to put his
two cents in.

"You ought to know all about backshooting, Mc-
Masters. That's how you got your rep," he said. "Well,
look to yourself, that's all I got to say. Them Winslows
was friends of mine, and I ain't forgetting how you did
them. Shooting and burning them, even the womenfolk!"

"A friend of the Winslows?" Boyd said.

"You're damned right!"

"Then you must die."

"I—*what*?!"

"I'm going to kill you," Boyd said.

He pushed back his chair, stood up. "No man who sided with those scum walks away from me alive. Go for your gun."

Nacker tried to regain some of his bluster. "You ain't impressing no one with your big bluff."

"Go for your gun."

Nacker sneered. "Going to take on all three of us?"

But Panamint and Skraggs were already edging away from him.

"Your friends don't think it's a bluff," Kingston said.

He was pleasant, almost merry, with a twinkle in his eye. His hands were still folded on the table.

He said, "You came spoiling for a fight, and now you've got one."

Nacker's sneer crumbled. His eyes darted this way and that, seeking a way out.

"Y-you keep pushing, McMasters, you're gonna push me too far!"

"I'll count to three, Nacker."

"I ain't scared of you."

Panamint chewed his lips. "There'll be no fight. Walk away, Nacker."

"Move, and I'll kill you where you stand, Nacker," Boyd said.

"Get going, Nacker," Panamint said.

"He means it," Nacker said.

Skraggs bristled. "Hell, Panamint! Why should we

crawfish for this son of a bitch?''

"Jeff said—"

"I don't back off on his say-so or any other man's!''

"That's telling him, Clete," Kingston said.

"Nobody ast' yew.''

Panamint groaned. "You're playing right into their hands!''

"I don't want you," Boyd said. "Just Nacker.''

"I'm going," Panamint said.

Skraggs frowned. His mouth worked, as if trying to get rid of a bitter taste. "Never thought I'd see yew losin' your guts," he said.

"I've got brains enough to follow orders," Panamint said. "Jeff said no shooting. If you get through this, he'll skin you alive.''

Nacker said, "It ain't right, you running out on me.''

"You coming, Skraggs?''

"Waal . . .''

Skraggs started backing away.

"It ain't right," Nacker said.

"When you get to Hell, send the Winslows my regards," Boyd said *"One!"*

"Damn you," Nacker said.

"Two!"

"All right, you bastard!''

Not waiting for the count of three, Nacker went for his gun. Before it cleared the holster, there were two shots.

One took Nacker in the heart. It came from Boyd's gun. The other hit Clete Skraggs square in the middle of the forehead. It came from the smoking derringer in Kingston's hand. He must have palmed it at first sight of the trio, concealing it beneath his folded hands while he bided his time.

Not until the last echoes of gunfire faded away did the crowd react. Then came the uproar.

Panamint stood with his hands raised, palms out. His complexion was green-tinged.

"Any complaints?" Boyd said.

Panamint shook his head, neck creaking with tension.

"Take a message to your boss," Boyd said. "Rustling's finished in Sinagua County. The smart ones will get out now. Tomorrow will be too late.

"That's all. You can go."

Panamint hesitated. "You—you wouldn't shoot me in the back, would you?"

"I'd shoot you in the front, if I wanted to. What happened between Nacker and me was personal. The same will happen to anybody that speaks up for that Winslow trash. You're safe now, but don't let me see you tomorrow."

"What about him?" Panamint said, meaning Kingston.

"He won't shoot, will you, Kingston?"

"Only in self-defense," Kingston said.

"Like you did with Clete?" Panamint said.

"That's right."

"He wasn't reaching."

"No? Looked that way to me. Of course, if you'd care to press the point . . ."

"I'm going," Panamint said. He asked Boyd, "Can I go?"

"I'm sick of looking at you," Boyd said. "Git!"

Not once from the time of the shooting had Panamint

taken his eyes from the leveled guns of Kingston and Boyd, not even to glance at his two companions sprawled dead on the floor.

Still not looking at them, he edged around the bodies and made for the exit, keeping his hands up. He moved jerkily, in fits and starts, like a bug that's been swatted but not squashed.

Tom Krang, the Fighting Barkeep, stood behind the long bar, cradling a sawed-off shotgun. Panamint passed him as if walking on eggs. Krang made a face, shouting, "Boo!"

Panamint squawked, jumped, triggering scattered laughs from the crowd. He scurried toward the double doors. As he was going out, in came LaRue and Olcott. Panamint squeezed past them, vanishing into the night.

LaRue said, "What's going on here?"

"Nothing, Sheriff, just a couple of killings, that's all," Tom Krang said.

The lawmen eyed the bodies.

"It's Skraggs and Nacker," LaRue said, disturbed. "This is a bad business, a bad business."

Clete Skraggs, unlovely in life, looked worse in death. Olcott, toeing the corpse, smirked.

"Now, ain't that a dirty shame," he said. "He cheated the hangman but not justice."

"It's a powder keg," LaRue said, giving Olcott a dirty look for his levity. "What a time for this to happen, with that Rock House crowd in town!"

"Trouble follows them. Looks like it caught up with these two," Olcott said.

"We'd better get this straightened out pronto," LaRue said.

"Good idea, Sheriff," Kingston said. "And how about getting those bodies out of here? They're starting to stink up the place."

LaRue crossed to the table where Kingston sat. Boyd stood beside it, his gun holstered, thumbs hooked into the corners of his pockets.

LaRue said, "I might have known you'd be mixed up in all this, Kingston. This your handiwork?"

"I killed Clete." Kingston indicated Boyd. "He did for Nacker."

"Who, Bowman?"

"I don't know who he is. The deceased had some crazy idea his name was McMasters, that he was some kind of troubleshooter for the Cattleman's Protection Association."

"*What!*" Shaken, LaRue demanded, "Is this true?"

"As far as it goes," Boyd said.

"What the hell!"

Olcott chuckled. "If that don't beat all!"

LaRue said, "You've got some explaining to do, whatever your name is."

"McMasters, Boyd McMasters."

"What's 'Frank Bowman' then, your alias?"

"One name's as good as another when your own won't do."

"You're an Association man?"

"That's right."

"I suppose you can prove it?"

"That's right."

"I've got a good mind to lock you up!" LaRue roared.

"There's no law against a man going by any name he likes."

Olcott said, "He's got you there, Sheriff."

"There's a law against murder!"

"Self-defense," Kingston said, "a clear-cut case. I'll swear to it on a stack of bibles."

"Oh, you will, will you?" LaRue said.

"Them boys came in here looking for trouble—you know how they are. Were," Kingston corrected. "Nacker knew McMasters for an Association man. Those Rock House boys ain't overly fond of that outfit, so they called him on it."

"And?"

"That's it."

"Where do you fit into this, Kingston?"

"Just an innocent bystander."

"Innocent? You killed Skraggs!"

"I was afraid he was going to kill me. A clear-cut case of self-defense, Sheriff. Two clear-cut cases."

"I suppose you can prove it?"

"A dozen witnesses will swear to it. Hell, two dozen."

"All friends and associates of yours, I'm sure."

"You can't expect my enemies to take my part," Kingston said.

Tom Krang shouted across the floor, "That's how it happened, Sheriff! I saw the whole thing!"

"So did we," a voice said.

It had depth, timbre, and projection, cutting across the hubbub of background noise and chatter. The voice of a trained speaker. The voice of Oates Hull.

He stood on the middle of the staircase, flanked by

his brothers, Porter and Courtney. All wore black hats and black swallowtail coats. Oates wore a richly patterned vest, adorned by the thick gold chain of a watch fob. Courtney was even more dandified, with brilliantined hair, waxed mustache, and knife-creased trousers. Porter's fair hair spilled over his broad shoulders. His gunbelt was old, worn. His trousers were tucked into the tops of his boots.

The trio paused for an instant, as if self-consciously holding the pose to maximize its theatricality. Oates nodded, and they descended the stairs.

They crossed to where the bodies lay. Oates served as spokesman. Acknowledging LaRue with a nod, he said, "Sheriff."

"Marshal," LaRue said.

"No need for you to trouble yourself about this." Oates made a flicking gesture toward the corpses, as if he were referring to the merest trifle.

"No trouble at all," LaRue said. "It's my job."

"Not after election day," Courtney Hull said.

"The voters will decide that. In the meantime, I don't see any reason to play politics with the law," LaRue said.

Courtney started to reply, but Oates motioned him to silence.

"I quite agree," Oates said. "But the fact of the matter is that justice has been served."

"That how you see it?"

"That's how the law sees it. There's no crime in a fair fight. That's what this was, a fair fight."

Porter said loudly, "Anybody see it different?"

No one spoke up with a contradictory view.

Oates Hull smiled, holding his hands palms-up. "I rest my case."

"The Rock House crowd won't like this," LaRue said.

"Their likes and dislikes are a matter of total indifference to me. Of course, I understand your solicitude for their welfare, considering that they're an important part of your constituency. But every right-thinking citizen in this community will rejoice at the removal of two such vicious malefactors from our midst."

"They won't be so happy when the bullets start flying."

"Depends on which way they're flying," Porter Hull said.

LaRue turned to face him. "My job is to keep the peace, not start a war."

"Then do your job. If Parry acts up, crack down on him—hard. If you don't, we will."

"That a threat?"

"Take it anyway you like."

LaRue smiled grimly. "You're trying to browbeat the duly elected sheriff of this county. That's an insult to the office, and to the good citizens who place their trust in it."

Oates nodded agreeably, as if conceding LaRue a point. "What brother Porter is trying to say, in his rough but honest way, is that violence and lawlessness have been tolerated for too long in these parts. The source of that contagion is the robbers' roost known as Rock House. Rustling, banditry, murder—it must and shall stop! The public demands action!"

"Hear, hear!" cried members of the Hull claque, scattered throughout the crowd.

LaRue said, "Show me evidence that Parry's gang has committed any of those crimes, and I'll arrest them on the spot."

"Instead of persecuting honest citizens for defending themselves, your time would be better spent riding herd on the outlaw gang," Oates said.

LaRue laughed. He asked Boyd, "You call sneaking around under a false flag 'honest'?"

"I don't show my cards until all the bets are on the table," Boyd said.

"Sure, sure. And you, Kingston—I recollect a time, not so very long ago, when you and Skraggs and Osmond were thick as thieves."

"I'm sure you meant that as a figure of speech, Sheriff," Kingston said. "I was just stringing them on, giving them enough rope to see if I could learn their plans."

LaRue didn't try to hide his skepticism. "Got an answer for everything, don't you?"

Kingston shrugged. At that moment, Doc Grinnell bustled in through the front door, black bag in hand. His head and shoulders were wet. Outside, it had started to rain.

He glanced at the bodies. "Nice shooting. Who's wounded?"

"Nobody, Doc," Olcott said.

"Dammit, I told you not to send for me when they're dead!"

Kingston said, "Sorry you were dragged out for nothing, Doc. Just so it won't be a total loss, have a drink on the house."

"I'll have *two* drinks, thank you very much!" Grinnell snapped.

"You're a wonder, Doc. Full of piss and vinegar, God bless you," Kingston said. "In fact, I'm buying for everyone! Belly up to the bar and name your poison, boys!"

The invitation met with a roar of approval and a rush to the bar.

"That includes you too, Sheriff, and your deputy," Kingston said. "The whiskey's good, no matter who's buying!"

"Since you put it that way, don't mind if I do," LaRue said.

"That's the spirit!"

Oates Hull harumphed. "Then we can consider the matter closed, LaRue?"

"There'll have to be an inquest, but that's just a formality. I wash my hands of the whole business."

"Fine, fine."

"But Parry won't be so obliging."

Porter Hull said, "You're liable to be holding an inquest on him pretty soon."

"With that attitude, there's liable to be a whole lot of inquests," LaRue said. "The Reebs can't supply coffins fast enough to meet the demand as it is."

"Must hurt to lose all those registered voters on your side."

"Oh, I suspect the balance will even out, by and by," LaRue said. "Believe I'll have that drink now. Good night, Marshal."

"Sheriff," Oates said.

LaRue started off, paused, and said, "Bowman?—

McMasters?—whatever your name is, don't leave town before the inquest.''

"Leave? Just when things are getting interesting? Not a chance!''

"I want to have a long talk with you.''

"I'll be around.''

"Do that. Coming, Olcott?''

"Be with you in a minute, Sheriff.''

LaRue crossed to the bar, exchanging greetings with Grinnell. Kingston shouted across the room, ''Best in the house for the sheriff, Tom!''

"Right!'' Tom Krang stood on tiptoes, shouting over the tops of the heads of those crowding the bar.

"And get rid of these carcasses!''

Tom Krang flashed Kingston a sign of acknowledgment. A moment later, a pair of large men presented themselves front and center.

The senior man said, ''Where do you want the stiffs?''

"Out of here,'' Kingston said.

Oates Hull said, ''They'll have to go to the undertakers.''

The senior man said doubtfully, ''That's a long way off, Marshal.''

"It's raining too,'' the junior man added.

Kingston said, ''Let the undertaker come for them. Why should you boys do all the work.''

"Thanks, Kip,'' the senior man said.

"But get them out of here. They stink.''

"Where should we put them?''

Porter Hull said, ''Put them out front. Lean them against a wall or something.''

Courtney laughed. "That'll be good advertising for the place!"

Kingston said, "Better set a lookout too, in case company's coming, if you catch my drift."

"I already did," Porter said. "There's two of them on the roof. With Winchesters."

"Good," Kingston said. "Take 'em away, boys."

The men picked up Skraggs by the arms and legs and carried him out the front door.

Olcott, sidling up beside Boyd, said out of the corner of his mouth, "What about the gold?"

"Later," Boyd said.

The men returned, hefted Nacker, and carried him away.

In a normal tone of voice, Olcott wondered, "How come you killed him?"

"For auld lang syne," Boyd said.

Olcott, puzzled, scratched his head.

The men returned, faces slick with rainwater and sweat. Kingston said, "Clean the stains off the floor and buy yourselves a drink."

They went to work. Kingston said, "Something I can do for you, Deputy?"

Olcott cleared his throat. "I never had much use for you, Kingston."

"Thanks!"

"But anybody who plugged Clete Skraggs can't be all bad. I'd have done it myself, but you beat me to it."

"That's right, he killed your friend Randle, didn't he?"

"One of the gang did. Two are dead, the third's in jail, and the fourth's running out of time."

"Do you know who he is?"

"Yard does."

"Has he talked?"

"He will. He wasn't very talkative, the last I saw of him." Olcott laughed nastily. "You can't beat the truth out of an unconscious man. When he comes to, I'll have another go-round with him. He'll talk."

"Might as well have a drink while you're waiting."

"Not a bad idea."

"Drink up, it's on the house."

"Okay," Olcott said.

Oxlike, feet dragging, he lumbered toward the bar. He didn't want to let Boyd out of his sight, but he couldn't stick around any longer without attracting attention.

"First lawman I ever saw who didn't jump at a free drink," Kingston said.

"He's got other things on his mind, like whomping Yard some more," Boyd said.

"Like you did Nacker?"

"That's different. Well, maybe not so different."

"You really killed him because he was a friend of those Winslows?"

"I killed him because he said he was a friend of theirs."

Kingston whistled soundlessly. "You must have a really big hate on for them."

"They did me a hurting once. I'm still touchy about it."

"I'll say!"

"What did Skraggs do to make you kill him?"

"Well, I'll tell you. I used to run with some of those Rock House boys once, way back when. Then I fell in with the Hulls. Porter mostly. We helped each other out of a couple of scrapes. He's just about the best friend I've got. I get along pretty good with Court too. Oates, he's too much of a politician to have much liking for my kind, but we tolerate each other on account of the others.''

''And he don't mind having your gun siding him.''

''That too,'' Kingston said. ''You've been in Smoke Tree long enough to see the way of it. The Hulls and the Rock House gang are sure to fight sooner or later. I've been sitting on the fence, but when push comes to shove, I'll come down on the side of the Hulls. Tonight, push came to shove.

''The question is, which side will you come down on, McMasters?''

''The ranchers' side,'' Boyd said. ''As long as they're Association members, that is.''

Kingston nodded. ''That puts you head-on against Parry.''

''You figure that makes us allies?''

''Why not?''

''I'll think about it,'' Boyd said.

''Don't wait too long to make up your mind,'' Kingston said. ''I've got a feeling that things are going to happen fast.''

A tremendous blast rocked the night, a crashing chaos of roaring noise. Walls shook, windows shattered. A thunderclap, an artillery barrage, an earthquake—all seemed combined in a concussion which rose to a hammering peak.

The blast spent its force, muted, and rolled away.

As the last rumbles died down, Boyd said, ''Sounds like things are happening already!''

Nine

The jail was a smoldering pile of rubble.

"Whoever the dynamiter is, he don't do things by halves," Boyd said.

He was talking to himself. He stood in the shadows, watching the scene at the jail—what was left of it. It looked like an overturned ant mound. The people scurrying around it were the ants.

LaRue and Olcott led the rescue attempt. There wasn't much they could do. The rock pile was hot. That was all that was left of the jail, a rock pile, a heap of round stones like scorched skulls.

The volunteer fire brigade was there. Most of their efforts were devoted to putting out the numerous small fires started by flaming debris that had rained down on neighboring rooftops. A good thing that the jail had stood alone on its section of Burnett Street, west of Grand, for any adjacent buildings would surely have been destroyed by the blast.

Crowds of the curious ringed the site, kept back by the heat and the fear that some unexploded bundles of dynamite still lurked in the rubble. The hot spot glowed orange.

The fire brigade set to with their hand pumps, spouting streams of water on the hot rocks. Clouds of steam rose, hissing like a kingdom of snakes.

Boyd stood in the mouth of an alley on the north side of Mercado Street, not far from the barbershop and Wells Fargo office. Show himself in the light, where a sniper could pick him off? Not a chance. East Burnett Street was the site of the Doghouse Bar, the Parry gang's favorite watering hole.

As the rubble cooled, rescue workers with long-handled prybars poked among the stones, searching for bodies. No one inside the jail could have survived the blast.

A hand jutted out of a mound of debris. Rescuers set about unearthing its owner. An arm and shoulder were revealed. A man took hold of the arm with both hands and pulled, trying to haul the body free. The arm came off, causing the man to take a fall, still clutching the arm. With a shout, he flung it from him.

When the excitement died down, the diggers went back to work, slowly and more carefully. The body was brought to light, identified as Chris Yard.

Boyd had been wondering if Yard had been in jail at the time of the blast, or if it was all a ruse to cloak his escape.

"That settles that," he said.

The diggers kept working, probing for the remains of Joslyn and the others who had been guarding the jail. Boyd had seen enough. He went back to the hotel, keeping to the lots and alleys, shunning well-lit open spaces.

The Majestic lobby was empty, hushed, the lamps lit low. The night clerk was Reg, the ancient bellman. He sat slumped with his arms folded on the marble-topped desk, head resting on his hands. He might have been asleep, or dead. Except for his eyes, watery slits that fastened on Boyd when he came through the front door, tracking his progress across the carpeted floor.

The bellman stirred, sitting up with a dry rustling. Crooking a sticklike finger, he beckoned to Boyd.

Boyd changed course, went to the desk. The bell-man shoved a sealed envelope at him.

"For you," he said.

"Who's it from?" Boyd said.

The bellman's head sank into his hands, his eyes closing. Boyd shrugged, slapped a coin on the counter, and went to the stairs.

Pausing at the foot of the stairs, he looked back over his shoulder. The bellman seemed not to have moved, but the coin was gone.

Boyd opened the envelope. Inside was a note. Printed in block letters was: "COME TO ROOM 206."

Room 206 was on the west side of the hotel, facing Grand Street. The second floor was dim, quiet. So was the third. Boyd explored both, making sure they were free of lurkers before going to Room 206.

Standing to one side, protected by the wall, he knocked on the door. He used his gun, tapping the muzzle gently against the door panel.

From the other side, a muffled voice: "Who's there?"

"The man with the note," Boyd said.

The bolt was thrown, the door unlocked and opened a crack. Boyd used the toe of his boot to push it inward. He peeked around the doorjamb, ready to duck back at a sign of danger.

The door opened on a small wood-paneled anteroom. Standing in a corner with her back to the wall was Delores. She held a leveled gun—not a lady's pistol, but a big .44.

"I've got one too," Boyd said.

He showed it to her. She lowered her gun to her side.

"Come in," she said.

He entered, stepping to the side to avoid being outlined in the doorway. Reaching behind him, he closed the door. His gun was still leveled.

"I had to be sure it was you," she said.

"It's me."

"Perhaps you'll feel better if I set down the gun."

"It couldn't hurt," Boyd said.

She put the gun on a round-topped table covered by a lace shawl and stepped away from it. "Lock the door."

He did so. "Mind if I look around?"

"Go ahead."

"Ladies first," he said, gesturing with the gun.

She shrugged, going through the doorway he had indicated. He picked up her gun, not wanting to leave it around unattended.

Room 206 was actually a suite of rooms. Beyond

the anteroom lay a parlor, with heavy overstuffed furniture. To the right, a curtained archway led into a bedroom. Boyd searched them all, and the closets too.

"Don't forget to look under the bed," she said.

"I won't."

No one was hiding under the bed. There were no connecting doors to adjacent rooms. He liked that. Outside the windows was a balcony. He didn't like that so well, even though it was empty.

"Suspicious man," Delores said.

"Cautious."

"That is good."

They were in the parlor. He unloaded her gun, set it aside, and sat down in a wingbacked armchair.

"Alone at last," he said, "but for how long?"

"I wonder about that myself. Not too long, perhaps. So we must speak plainly, McMasters."

"The name on the register is Bowman."

"News travels fast in a town such as this. By now, there are few in Smoke Tree who do not know who you are—what you are."

"What's that?"

"A *pistolero*."

"And what are you?"

"A whore."

"Well, now, don't be too hard on yourself."

"You find me attractive?"

She was beautiful.

"You ain't ugly," he said.

"Men desire me. I give them what they want, and they give me what I want. That's how I got this suite, my job in the hotel, the clothes on my back, and the rings on my fingers.''

"Sounds like you're doing all right for yourself."

She smiled bitterly. "You know who owns the hotel? Dunston. He keeps me, for when he comes into town. What do you say to that?"

"I'd say it's a hard dollar. I've met the man."

"You are not without understanding."

"It ain't Dunston who's got you in fear for your life, though."

"No. He cares for me, in his way."

"Why not go to him? He'll protect you."

"I will—if I live through this night."

"Which is where I come in," Boyd said.

She crossed to a sideboard, where a cut-glass crystal decanter sat on a sterling silver tray. "Do you want some brandy? It's very good."

"If you're joining me," Boyd said.

She filled two glasses, handed him one, and sipped from the other. "So you can see it's not poisoned," she said.

He drank. It was good. He said so. When his glass was drained, she asked if he wanted some more.

"I'm fine, thanks," he said.

"Then let's go to bed."

He shook his head, half-amazed, half-admiring. "Lady, I thought I was a fast worker, but you've got me beat by a country mile!"

"Don't you want to make love to me?"

"Hell, yes!"

"Don't waste time. There's no telling when they'll come for me."

"I want some answers first."

"You'll get them. Later."

Her hair was bound up, pinned tightly to the top of her head. She loosened it, letting it fall free, a glossy black mane reaching past her shoulders.

She wore a black satin dress, with black lace at the collar and cuffs. It covered her from neck to ankle, but was intricately constructed to display her superb physique.

Boyd reached for her, embracing her, pulling her to him. Her mouth was hot and sweet. He caressed her, feeling the soft padded flesh beneath the satin. His hands ran up and down her. She leaned into him, grinding against his hardness.

When he came up for air, he said, "What the hell, we can always talk afterward."

He scooped her up, sweeping her off her feet. She knotted her fingers at the back of his neck. He carried her into the bedroom, to the big brass bed.

He tossed his hat on a chair, hung his gunbelt on the brass bedstead. He peeled off his shirt. Delores sat up in bed, nimble fingers undoing the complicated buttons and hooks and fasteners that held her garment together. While she was occupied, Boyd plucked his second gun from the top of his waistband, covered it with the shirt, and placed it on the floor beside the bed.

Delores pulled the dress down to her waist. She was cinched into a kind of corset that laced up the back. It had black lace panels and pushed up her breasts. Her skin was tawny gold, with a metallic sheen. Her nipples were dark brown, pert, uptilted.

Boyd stroked her, easing her on to her back. He gripped her dress with both hands, shucking it down her hips and off her. She wore red silk drawers, garters, black stockings. He took down her drawers.

Strapped to the top of her right thigh, running along the outside of her leg, was a sheath containing the silver dagger.

"I was wondering where you kept that," he said.

He took it off and dropped it on top of his shirt. He stood at the bedside. She crouched on the bed facing him, her long legs folded under her. Her loins were pale gold and her bush a glossy black pelt. She held his hips and rubbed her face against his crotch. He peeled down his jeans, freeing his hardness. It flopped in front of her face. She held it in both hands, guiding it into her mouth. . . .

He wanted her all the way. She lay on her back and he mounted her. As he entered her, she thrust up her hips to meet him.

She was a hell of a woman: beautiful, passionate, shameless. Boyd only wished that he could have given her his full attention instead of being distracted by waiting for the approach of her killers.

Still, he made the best of it. The fires of her flesh banished for a time the hateful memories of the inferno that haunted his every moment, night and day: the holocaust of his West Texas ranch house with his screaming wife Hannah burning alive inside it while he stood by, helpless to save her.

The Winslows had done that. He'd paid them back in coin, killing and burning them, their whores, property, livestock, everything. He thought he'd put some distance between him and the hurt, until Nacker had reminded him just how close it still was. . . .

It was midway between midnight and dawn, the dead-night hour. Delores and Boyd lay side by side in bed, naked under the sheets. The room was thick with shadows.

"They will come soon, I think," Delores said.

Boyd was ready for them. "Seaton won't come himself. He'll send others."

A sudden sharp intake of breath, swiftly stifled.

"So. You know," she said.

"Most of it. The rest I can guess."

She lay on her side, facing him. "Tell me what you know. What you *think* you know."

"Seaton planned to rob his own mine. Well, not his mine. He's the manager, not the owner. A glorified hired man, but a hired man all the same, subject to being fired at the whim of his bosses. He decided to feather his own nest. Somewhere along the line, he was indiscreet. Maybe he planned to run away with you, or maybe he talked out of turn. That doesn't matter. What's important is that you found out, and made plans of your own, plans that didn't include him. He waited for the company to make a big gold shipment, but you moved first. That's where Kingston comes in.

"You passed the word to Kingston. He rounded up some of his old Rock House pards: Osmond, Skraggs, and Yard. They jumped the stagecoach at North Pass. I don't know where Butch Randle fits in. Maybe he knew too much and had to die, or maybe somebody got just got trigger-happy. It was all for nothing, though, because they didn't get the gold. Kingston hightailed it back to town, Yard and Skraggs scattered. Osmond was wounded and couldn't run, so they left him behind with a bullet in the brain so he couldn't talk.

"Kingston got through by the skin of his teeth. He switched horses in time to join the posse chasing the gang he'd been a part of. I bet that gave him a laugh. Seaton was spooked by almost having the gold snatched out of his jaws. He made his move when the posse left town. He had the combination to the mining company safe. All he had to do was walk in and take the gold. He blew up the vault, trying to make it look like the gold had been blown up too. The mining guard, Craigie, was killed to protect the secret."

The killers had arrived. Small betraying noises, swift blurred shadows, had given them away. Damned few men could sneak up on a man like Boyd, whose every sense was keenly pitched to detect the slightest subtle alteration in his surroundings.

He kept talking, going on as if he hadn't heard a thing.

He said, "It was just coincidence that I got tangled up with the robbers. Or maybe not. They were rustlers too, and that's my meat, so we were bound to lock horns. The funny thing is, I didn't care about the gold, but nobody believed me."

"Can you blame them?" Delores said.

"No. The gold drove everyone wild. Skraggs and Kingston fell out. Seaton must have guessed that you crossed him. That explains that little scene in the dining room tonight. Seaton blew up Yard, to keep him from telling what he knew. He's tying up all his loose ends. You're one of them, Delores. That's why you've got to die."

Two killers, on the balcony.

"Who can you go to for help, Delores? Not the law. Not Kingston. You can't be sure he's not tying up loose ends too. Dunston's out of town. That leaves me."

The gun was in his hand. He'd picked it up earlier, after the loving. It lay by his side, covered by a sheet.

He squeezed her thigh with his free hand, the one not holding the gun.

"Don't worry, Delores. Your secrets are safe with me. I'm a stock detective, not a lawman. I've got a hunch your problems will be solved sooner than you think."

"I'm not sure I like the sound of that."

Glass broke—a window in the parlor. A diversion. A shadow appeared on the bedroom window, the shadow of a gunman. Boyd shot it, through the sheet. The bullet went through the glass, into the gunman. The glass shattered, spraying outward.

Boyd rolled out of bed, got his feet under him on the floor, sprang toward the window. The man he'd shot lay sprawled against the balcony railing, dead, shrouded with glittering glass fragments.

The second man crouched in front of the parlor window he'd broken, gun in hand. He fired at Boyd, missed. Boyd didn't.

Two shots, two kills.

The man outside the bedroom window was the lean-faced character Boyd had seen driving the mining company wagon. The other was Hardrock Riley, his hairless skull gleaming like a pale moon. Below the brows his face was a horror, where Boyd's bullet had hit it.

Ten

The day of the Big .70 had come.

It was a gray day, damp and gloomy. The mid-morning funeral of Fyfe and Jess was about to begin. Dunston and his men were massed in the graveyard, clustered around two fresh holes in the ground. Their horses were nearby, tethered to an iron spear fence in a weedy unused corner of the lot.

Two coffins, their wood raw and yellow, stood on sawhorse trestles near the graves. The hearse wagon, which had delivered them, stood off to one side, its horse team outfitted with mournful black plumes. Beside it stood two black-clad characters in stovepipe hats, keeping to themselves.

No gravediggers were present, and no preacher. The graves had been dug by Dunston's men, who would be doing the burying later. Dunston himself would say words over the departed. Tucked under his arm was a leather-bound family bible; strapped onto his hips was

a pair of six-guns. The rest of the funeral party was
outfitted like a war party. Picketed on the hilltop were
two sentries with Winchesters.

In town, a gang of men came out of the Doghouse
Bar, mounted up, and rode toward the graveyard. Jeff
Parry, his gang, and assorted hardcases who had come
in for the showdown. Fifteen men.

They came on slow, steady, and deliberate, as if they
had all the time in the world.

Maybe they did. They were killers all, while Dunston's men were mostly cowboys. A few had done their
share of killing, including Dunston and his foreman,
Bonner, but the majority lacked the true killer instinct.

Dunston had an ace up his sleeve. Scattered in among
his men, disguised in cowboy clothes and oversized hats,
were the Hulls and Kip Kingston. That evened the odds.

Boyd had a bird's-eye view of the showdown. He was
perched in the belfry of the church steeple overlooking
the graveyard.

He'd come there early, before dawn, toting the carrying case he'd redeemed from the hotel storeroom. The
church door had been unlocked. He'd climbed to the top
of the tower and set up shop.

The outlaws were at the foot of the graveyard hill,
skirting it in a loose ragged line. They sat their horses,
waiting. Dunston's men were on foot. There were advantages and disadvantages to both tactics. A mounted
charge carried great force, but it was harder to shoot
accurately from horseback. That would not necessarily
hamper Parry and his top guns, who were veteran pistol
fighters, but it would handicap the others. Dunston's
men had the high ground, and a more stable shooting

platform, but could they withstand the charge?

The question was about to be decided.

Boyd scanned the scene with his binoculars, frowning. Something was wrong. Parry was missing some of his best men. Where were Concho, Lake, Rollin, and Martinez?

They weren't lurking in the thickets, planning a sneak attack. Boyd had been the first on the scene, and no one had slipped by him.

Dunston and Parry shouted challenges at each other. The wind carried their words away, but Boyd didn't need to hear them. Their meaning was clear: *This is the showdown.*

When the shooting started, Parry would be the first to die.

Boyd readied his long rifle. Big .70. Nestled in the breech of the octagonal barrel was a hand-loaded round, its soft nose tipped by a brass carpet tack. When it hit, the fragmenting lead would drive that tack with pile-driver force.

This wasn't sportsmanship. He wasn't hunting big game. He was killing men.

Mounted on the rifle was a telescopic sight, not that he needed it at this close distance.

Parry was stalling, delaying the fight. Why? What was he waiting for?

That sixth sense was warning Boyd of imminent disaster. He eased off the trigger for a final look-see. Just when he had convinced himself he was imagining things, he saw something that shouldn't be.

The undertakers were drawing guns!

They shot the hilltop sentries, mowing them down.

Not undertakers at all, but Parry's men!

He'd taken them for granted, and so had Dunston. Who looks twice at an undertaker? They weren't the Reebs, of course, but he'd just assumed that the brothers had declined the opportunity to attend a six-gun funeral and sent assistants in their place.

Now that he thought of it, the "undertakers" had arrived before Dunston's group, unloaded the coffins, gone to the sidelines, and stayed there, ignored and unnoticed as the mourners arrived.

Their opening shots signaled Parry's charge. The outlaws spurred their horses, sweeping up the hill into the graveyard.

The undertakers swung their guns downhill. Dunston was a dead man, unless—

The Big .70 roared.

Crashing like thunder, it punched a hole in the nearest undertaker.

Ejecting the spent shell, Boyd fed a fresh round into the breech.

Thunder hammered again, letting daylight into the second funereal gunman.

The battle was crackling now, a melee. Cowboys crouched behind tombstones, shooting and being shot by charging outlaws.

The rear door of the hearse crashed open, and a nimble gunman leaped out. He was dead before he hit the ground—blasted by Boyd's long rifle.

Kingston shot at Parry, missed. Parry's horse upreared, standing on its hind legs. A forehoof struck Kingston, knocking him down. Parry leaned around the horse's neck and shot him. Kingston was torn, trampled.

Parry made for Dunston. The cattle baron had lost his hat, baring his distinctive shot of white hair.

Dunston fired at Parry, missed. He dodged, scrambling for cover as Parry came on. A bullet struck his leg, knocking it out from under him. Dunston fell sideways, tumbling into an open grave.

The Big .70 combined with the Hulls' deadly firepower to thin the outlaw ranks.

Parry halted beside the open grave. At the bottom lay Dunston, winded, wounded, stunned, yet aware enough to know that this was his finish.

Dunston was unarmed, his gun lost in the fall. He snarled defiance as Parry's big-bored gun swung in line with his head—

Thunder cracked.

Parry flew out of the saddle, toppling into the grave on top of Dunston. The outlaw had been cored like an apple by the Big .70.

The surviving gang members cut and ran. Boyd let them go. His job was done. Rustling was finished in Sinagua County—for now anyway.

The victors were not so charitably inclined. The cowboys' shooting was hit-and-miss, but not the Hulls'. Only a handful of outlaws managed to ride clear of the range of Hull guns.

The fight was done. Boyd eased off and took stock. Gunhawk Dale Mayfield would be disappointed when he finally arrived in Smoke Tree. There was no work for him to do.

No work, that is, but to use his talents to extend Dunston's domain. Power abhors a vacuum, and with the

rustlers gone, Dunston would seek to consolidate his su-
premacy.

Boyd had a solution to that. His knowledge of the
secret burial place of the two lynched men was a weapon
to curb Dunston's lust for power.

A speck crawled north on the road to the pass. Boyd
trained his binoculars on it: a lone man driving a wagon.
Seaton, taking advantage of the chaos to flee Smoke
Tree with his stolen gold.

Even with the telescopic sight, it was a long shot.

Boyd squeezed the trigger.

Seaton spasmed, as if struck by lightning. He flew off
the wagon, becoming one with the dirt.

The horses, spooked, ran faster, but they would stop
when they got tired.

Thunder boomed across the flat land, echoing to in-
finity.

Big .70.

Watch for

MEXICAN STANDOFF

5th in the exciting MCMASTERS series
from Jove

Coming in February!

*If you enjoyed this book,
subscribe now and get...*

TWO FREE

A $7.00 VALUE–

If you would like to read more of the very best, most exciting, adventurous, action-packed Westerns being published today, you'll want to subscribe to True Value's Western Home Subscription Service.

Each month the editors of True Value will select the 6 very best Westerns from America's leading publishers for special readers like you. You'll be able to preview these new titles as soon as they are published, *FREE* for ten days with no obligation!

TWO FREE BOOKS

When you subscribe, we'll send you your first month's shipment of the newest and best 6 Westerns for you to preview. With your first shipment, two of these books will be yours as our introductory gift to you absolutely *FREE* (a $7.00 value), regardless of what you decide to do. If

you like them, as much as we think you will, keep all six books but pay for just 4 at the low subscriber rate of just $2.75 each. If you decide to return them, keep 2 of the titles as our gift. No obligation.

Special Subscriber Savings

When you become a True Value subscriber you'll save money several ways. First, all regular monthly selections will be billed at the low subscriber price of just $2.75 each. That's at least a savings of $4.50 each month below the publishers price. Second, there is never any shipping, handling or other hidden charges—*Free home delivery*. What's more there is no minimum number of books you must buy, you may return any selection for full credit and you can cancel your subscription at any time. A TRUE VALUE!

A special offer for people who enjoy reading the best Westerns published today.

WESTERNS!

NO OBLIGATION

Mail the coupon below

To start your subscription and receive 2 FREE WESTERNS, fill out the coupon below and mail it today. We'll send your first shipment which includes 2 FREE BOOKS as soon as we receive it.

Mail To: **True Value Home Subscription Services, Inc. P.O. Box 5235
120 Brighton Road, Clifton, New Jersey 07015-5235**

YES! I want to start reviewing the very best Westerns being published today. Send me my first shipment of 6 Westerns for me to preview FREE for 10 days. If I decide to keep them, I'll pay for just 4 of the books at the low subscriber price of $2.75 each; a total $11.00 (a $21.00 value). Then each month I'll receive the 6 newest and best Westerns to preview Free for 10 days. If I'm not satisfied I may return them within 10 days and owe nothing. Otherwise I'll be billed at the special low subscriber rate of $2.75 each; a total of $16.50 (at least a $21.00 value) and save $4.50 off the publishers price. There are never any shipping, handling or other hidden charges. I understand I am under no obligation to purchase any number of books and I can cancel my subscription at any time, no questions asked. In any case the 2 FREE books are mine to keep.

Name
_____

Street Address _____ Apt. No. _____

City _____ State _____ Zip Code _____

Telephone _____

Signature _____
(if under 18 parent or guardian must sign)

Terms and prices subject to change. Orders subject
to acceptance by True Value Home Subscription
Services, Inc.

11765-X

THE SIZZLING NEW WESTERN SERIES
FROM THE CREATORS OF *LONGARM*

M^cMASTERS

Lee Morgan

Armed with a custom-built .70 caliber rifle, he is the law. To his friends, he is many things—a fighter, a lover, a legend. To his enemies, he is only one thing— the most dangerous man they have ever known.

__McMASTERS   0-515-11632-7/$4.99

__McMASTERS #2: SILVER CREEK SHOWDOWN
                                     0-515-11682-3/$3.99

__McMASTERS #3: PLUNDER VALLEY
                                     0-515-11731-5/$4.50

__McMASTERS #4: BIG .70   0-515-11765-X/$4.50

Payable in U.S. funds. No cash orders accepted. Postage & handling: $1.75 for one book, 75¢ for each additional. Maximum postage $5.50. Prices, postage and handling charges may change without notice. Visa, Amex, MasterCard call 1-800-788-6262, ext. 1, refer to ad # 555

Or, check above books and send this order form to:	Bill my:	☐ Visa ☐ MasterCard ☐ Amex	
The Berkley Publishing Group	Card#		(expires)
390 Murray Hill Pkwy., Dept. B			($15 minimum)
East Rutherford, NJ 07073	Signature		
Please allow 6 weeks for delivery.	Or enclosed is my:	☐ check ☐ money order	
Name		Book Total	$
Address		Postage & Handling	$
City		Applicable Sales Tax	$
State/ZIP		(NY, NJ, PA, CA, GST Can.) Total Amount Due	$